GW01117155

Bad In Bardino

Bad In Bardino

Nick Sweet

Clear Print Version
Copyright (C) 2016 Nick Sweet
Layout design and Copyright (C) 2019 by Next Chapter
Published 2019 by Gumshoe – A Next Chapter Imprint
Cover art by Cormarcovers.com
This book is a work of fiction. Names, characters, places, and incidents are the product of the author's imagination or are used fictiously. Any resemblance to actual events, locales, or persons, living or dead, is purely coincidental.
All rights reserved. No part of this book may be reproduced or transmitted in any form or by any means, electronic or mechanical, including photocopying, recording, or by any information storage and retrieval system, without the author's permission.
nicksweet1@hotmail.com

1

I was woken up by the sound of my mobile ringing. My head hurt and felt like it was about the size of a watermelon. I supposed that I might have had one or two too many the night before, as I sat up and grabbed the phone.
'Hello?'

'Is that Arthur Blakey, the private investigator?' a feminine voice asked.

'It is indeed.'

'Oh Mr. Blakey, I've heard that you are an expert when it comes to finding people, is that right?' Whoever she was, she spoke English with a foreign accent. Germanic, I should have said.

'Only when I manage to do it.'

'Do what?'

'Find them.'

'This is no laughing matter, Mr. Blakey.' She didn't seem to go for my line in humour. A lot of people don't, not that it's ever bothered me much.

'Never said it was.'

She went quiet for a moment and as I waited to hear what she was going to say next I could picture her in my mind's eye, or thought I could. I reckoned she was a pretty brunette. They often are, when I picture them. Not brunette necessarily, I don't mean, but pretty. I don't know why, but they just seem to come out that way. I suppose you could say I'm an optimist by nature. Maybe you have to be if you're going to last very long in my line of work. You get to see a lot of nasty stuff working as a private investigator, and you can't let it get to you. They should put having the ability to forget and bounce back from things in the job description.

Anyway, as I was saying, I pictured her as a pretty brunette, but kind of prim and proper in an old fashioned sort of way; and right now, I imagined how her brow might look as it furrowed in a cross expression. Then she said, 'Could you find somebody for me?'

'I could certainly try.'

'I should be most grateful if you would.'

I found her old-world tone of voice faintly amusing, or I would have done if my head hadn't been giving me so much grief. It must have been that last drink that did it, the last one or two, anyway. It or they were responsible for setting up the little arrangement the inside of my head currently appeared to be failing to enjoy with a rhythm section that featured some young skinhead thug on the drums. 'I shouldn't be too grateful,' I said. 'I don't come cheap.'

'How much?'

'Three hundred euros a day plus expenses,' I said. 'And another thousand if I find whoever it is I'll be looking for, half of which I get upfront.'

'And what if you don't find her?'

'You get the five hundred back.'

'I see…well that sounds reasonable,' she said. 'So you'll find her for me, then?'

'Find *who*?'

'My sister Gisela, Mr. Blakey… She's disappeared, you see.'

'I'd need a last name.'

'It's Schwartz.'

'And you are?'

'Inge,' she replied. 'Inge Schwartz.'

'Where are you now?'

'I'm in the street outside your office…the door is locked.'

'Yes, I've been called away,' I said. 'If you could come back in about an hour, I'll see you then.'

'Why so long?'

'There's a man I've been chasing and I've just caught up with him, only he's armed with a gun and–'

'Oh dear…do you want me to call the police?'

'No, I can handle it.'

'But it sounds as though this man is dangerous.'

'I can deal with him,' I said. Besides, I might have added, some of the cops in Bardino don't like me much, and I don't like them any better. But I decided to keep this last thought to myself. And anyway, I was only kidding her about chasing a man with a gun. Not that I don't chase armed men around a lot, because I do; only I wasn't doing so right then. What I was doing was sitting up in bed, having just woken up. 'Okay, well if you'd like to call round to my office in about an hour, I'll see you then,' I told her and hung up.

I looked at my watch. It had just turned half-past ten, which is late for some people to be lying in bed, perhaps, but par for the course for me when I'm not working. I'd just successfully solved a tricky murder investigation and made myself enough to last me for the next couple of months, so I was in no desperate hurry to find new clients. Of course if a suitable case came my way, then so much the better; but if it didn't, there was nothing to prevent me from sleeping late and enjoying a little time taking it easy.

I put my mobile back down on the bedside cabinet and scratched my head as I wondered what the sisters of nice Germanic girls were doing coming to places like Bardino and forgetting to call or write home. I was still wondering about this as I got dressed, then left the flat and headed for my office, which was just a few minutes' walk away, over on Calle Veracruz. I went in through the narrow doorway, which is squeezed in between a shop that sells watches on one side and a ladies' shoe shop on the other, then climbed the stairs. I took out my key and opened the door with the frosted glass window, bearing the legend ARTHUR BLAKEY, PRIVATE INVESTIGATOR, then entered. The solid oak desk was in that state of ordered perfection normally only achieved by the unemployed, and behind it the venetian blinds were partially drawn, so that the room was striped with shadow. There were two upright chairs on this side of the desk, and my more comfortable swivel number was on the other side. I went and sat in my chair and swiveled around on it a little as I waited for Inge Schwartz to show.

2

The very moment I opened the door to her, I realized I was all wrong about Inge Schwartz: she was no pretty brunette, not at all. She was a blonde, for a start.

'Perhaps you'd like to come in?' I said.

'Perhaps I would.'

I closed the door behind her and tried hard not to look her up and down too many times. I failed miserably in this, though, because she was a stunner. What's more, she knew it. She was honey blonde hair, neatly bobbed by an adept hand, tawny skin, china-blue eyes, red-painted bee-stung mouth, and bone structure that would have made Rodin throw away his chisel. She was slender in all the right places and less slender–in fact not slender *at all*–in all the right places, too, and she came wrapped in a fuchsia-coloured linen dress that she wore with a cream jacket of the same material and black court shoes.

She shrugged off her jacket and handed it to me like I was the doorman at some posh joint. The garment smelt of her perfume - Chanel No 5, if I wasn't mistaken. She said, 'I've brought some things for you.' She opened her handbag, a neat little Kelly number, took out an A3-sized manila envelope and handed it to me.

I took a look inside. There was a wad of money in it, as well as a photograph and a piece of paper. I took out the wad of money and riffled it. Then I counted it quickly and slipped it into the breast pocket of my jacket. Next I took out the photograph and had a look at it. It was a photograph of a girl of about eighteen or so. 'She looks a little like a younger version of you,' I said.

'We aren't sisters for nothing, Mr. Blakey.'

For a brief moment I was almost tempted to tell her she could dispense with the Mister business and just call me 'Art', short for 'Arthur', like everyone else I knew; but then I came to my senses and said instead, 'When was this photo taken?'

'Two or three years ago... it's the only one of her I could find.'

'How old is your sister now?'

'Twenty-one.'

I looked at the photograph. Her sister sure was a beautiful-looking girl. I took out the sheet of paper and examined it. It had been torn from a letter-writing pad, and so it shouldn't have surprised me, I don't suppose, to find that a letter had been written on it. What did surprise me, though, was the nature of the letter itself. I'm no graphologist, but the large spidery scrawl seemed decidedly childish to me, more like what a thirteen-year-old might produce than the sort of thing you'd expect from an adult, even a young one; and I noticed that none of the i's were dotted, which might suggest an absence of feelings of self-worth in the writer. Then there was the subject matter of the letter. It read like a young girl writing home from summer camp, where she was in the busy flurry of her first affair, and not at all like the letter of a young woman who had come to Bardino to live and then perhaps taken a wrong turning in her life and dropped out of contact. In short, there was an innocence bordering on outright childishness about the writing that struck me as a little odd, given that the date at the top of the page was June of this year.

'Please take a seat,' I said, and Miss Schwartz duly parked herself on one of the two upright chairs. She crossed her legs neatly at the knee, smoothed her dress down, and her foot kept time with some imaginary music that may or may not have been playing through her mind. From the expression on her face, though, music seemed to be the last thing she was concerned about.

'Is this letter the last you've heard from her?' I said as I sat in my padded swivel number.

She nodded and bit down on her lower lip, and for a terrible moment it looked like she might be about to break down in tears. Even while this was taking place, however, I continued to wonder whether I should believe what I was witnessing. Whether I could safely assume, in other words, that what I was seeing, or being permitted to watch, was in fact 'for real'.

I took a deep breath, puffed out my cheeks like a blowfish, and turned my attention back to the letter. Having taken note of the local address at the top of the page, I asked Miss Schwartz if she had called round to the place to see if her sister was still living there. She replied in the affirmative, shutting her eyes, as if she were being weighed down by heavy emotions. The person who was currently residing there, she explained, had told her that Gisela took off somewhere a couple of weeks ago. Where she'd gone and why, the man didn't know. Neither had he known when she was likely to return. All he'd been able to tell her was that she'd packed in her job and skipped town.

I figured that I would make the address, which was nearby as it happened, in the Bocanazo, my first port of call. Then I asked Miss Schwartz if she and Gisela had been brought up together and by the same parents; and if so, then where were they from? 'Yes,' was the answer to my first question, and 'Hamburg in Germany' her reply to the one that followed. I'd never been to the city and, beyond its geographical location, knew next to nothing about the place.

'So you will take the case?'

'I've taken your money, haven't I?'

'Do you think you can find my sister for me, Mr. Blakey?'

'Most probably…but what if she doesn't want to be found?'

'What on earth do you mean by that?'

'Imagine she's fallen in love with some lucky young brute and shacked up with him, but she doesn't want Daddy to find out.'

'Daddy passed away last year, sadly.'

'Well Mummy, then.'

'She died three years ago.'

'I'm sorry.'

'Don't be.'

'Do you have any other siblings?'

She shook her head and sighed, then took a delicate chew on her lower lip. 'It's not like her, to fail to write or call like this.'

'Did you have an argument with Gisela?'

'No.'

'How would you describe your relationship?'

'We were rather different.'

'Only you looked the same.'

'Similar, but not the same,' she corrected me.

That was true: while the girl in the photograph resembled the woman I was talking to, and indeed was clearly something of a stunner in her own right, her looks lacked the classical purity of those of her older sister. 'You didn't get along, then?'

'I never said that.'

'No, but you didn't say much.'

'I've always been the sensible one, Mr. Blakey, and Gisela just seemed to do exactly as she pleased.'

'So you resented her?'

'Stop putting words in my mouth,' she said. 'Anyway, it hardly matters how she and I got along, does it, if all I want is for you to find her?'

'It might matter a lot,' I replied, 'if you had an argument and she's decided not to talk to you anymore.'

'I can assure you that's not the case.'

'Is it possible you don't think it's the case but Gisela might?'

'No, but even if it was like that then I'd still want you to find her for me, just to know that she's all right.'

I took out my Parker and began to roll it between my fingers. 'What was Gisela doing in Bardino?'

'She was never the same after mother and father died.' Her brow furled like a coiled caterpillar. 'She was very close to them, you see.'

'Only to be expected, isn't it?' I said.

'Yes, but I mean…' She broke off, gripping her Kelly bag as if she thought somebody might be about to run off with it.

'I can see that you're upset, Mrs. Schwartz.'

'It's Miss.'

'Pardon me, *Miss* Schwartz,' I said. 'Can I get you a glass of water?'

She brushed my offer aside with a curt shake of the head.

'Something a little stronger then?'

'It's still morning,' she said, and regarded me with the sort of expression the headmistress of an expensive finishing school might reserve for the young man who has had the temerity to sneak into the girls' dormitory at night.

'You were saying how Gisela was very close to her parents…'

'Yes, she became depressed for a time after they died. Then once she'd snapped out of it, she came to Bardino with the intention of getting a job.'

'What sort of job?'

She shrugged. 'Waitressing or working in a hotel, something like that, I think.'

'Did she ever find any work?'

'I don't think so... not that she told me about, anyway.'

'Did she have much money?'

'She would have had some.'

'How much is some?'

'Well I'm not sure exactly,' she said. 'But what's all this got to do with anything, anyway? I want you to find my sister, not write a book about her.'

'I realize that.' I smiled, but you shouldn't read anything into that, because my smile is cheaper than chewing gum. Inge Schwartz blushed and looked away. I wondered if her blush was for real, or if it was all part of her act. I wondered which was cheaper, her blush or my smile, then said, 'But the more you can tell me about Gisela's lifestyle and situation, the easier it will make the job of finding her.'

'Well I've told you everything there is to tell.' She got to her feet as if she'd been ejected from the chair by a spring. 'I don't want to sit here taking up your time, Mr. Blakey, when you should be out there trying to find Gisela.'

She stopped when she got to the door and shot me an accusatory glance over her shoulder. 'You will let me know as soon as you find her, won't you?'

'I really don't know how you expect me to do that,' I said, 'if you haven't given me a number to call or an address where I can contact you.'

'Oh yes, how silly of me... you'd better have my mobile number.' She told me the number and I gave the Parker some work to do.

'And where are you staying right now?'

'In the hotel Las Palmeras.'

'Do you have a room number, or have you taken over the entire hotel?'

'Number four hundred and twenty three,' she said. 'And there's no need to be so snotty, is there?' She fixed me with her angry headmistress expression for a moment. 'Call me as soon as you know anything.'

'It will be my pleasure.'

Her eyes, which were as cold and beautiful as coral, raked me over as though she were considering whether to give me some kind of parting shot, but then she must have thought better of it because she opened the door and went out, leaving nothing but the subtle waft of Chanel No.5 and a thousand and one questions behind her.

3

I found the Porsche where I'd left it earlier and drove over to the Bocanazo, then parked round the back of the large sports complex there and walked to the block of flats where Gisela Schwartz had been living. It was four storeys tall and certainly nothing to write home about, which I figured might very well explain why the Schwartz girl had stopped doing just that. The block, like all the others, was designed so that it stood at forty-five degrees to the street; the walls were painted white and each flat had its own small balcony.

It was fairly quiet in the *barrio* right now, but that was only to be expected at this hour. Things could often have a way of livening up here after dark, though. I asked myself what was a girl from a nice German family doing living in a dump like this, as I entered the block.

I heard all sorts of noises as I climbed the stairs: a woman screamed at her child, who then must have picked up a smack because the next moment the child began to bawl. A man was yelling in some form of Arabic; and somewhere else, another man was yelling in what might have been Russian. As well as the shouting, there was a fair amount of cooking going on, so that I felt as though I were taking a lightning-fast tour through a number of nightmare holiday destinations.

The address I had for Gisela Schwartz was flat 4D, up on the top floor. I rang the buzzer and nobody came to open up, so I went back down and found my Porsche, then drove round to the front of the block and pulled up and waited behind the wheel. There was only the one way in and out of the building, and I was watching it, so I was bound to see her if and when she showed.

I waited for two hours, by which time the September sun was working up a temperature. A glance at my Swatch told me it was coming up to two in the afternoon, which is lunchtime in this part of the world. I might be an athletic kind of guy with the kind of build that makes me look good in the slim fitting summer suits I favour, but I do like to eat even so, and my belly was cranking out an overture on the theme of hunger. I went and parked myself at one of the several vacant tables, from which I had a perfect view of the only entrance to the block across the way, and asked for a *bocadillo* with *jamon serrano*, a dish of olives and a cold bottle of Cruzcampo. The waiter nodded and said '*Muy bien*' or 'very good'; then I took the photograph from my pocket and held it up. 'You recognize this girl?' I asked him.

He looked at the photo, then took it from me and studied it. 'Looks like the girl lives in the block over there.' He pointed with a stubby digit. 'Only she's younger here, in the photograph, no?'

'The photograph was taken two or three years ago.'

'Yeah, that's her.'

'You know anything about her?'

'Told me she's German,' he said. 'Sure speaks good, though.'

'Talks like one of the locals, does she?'

He shook his head. 'No, she speaks educated, not like us down here.' I'd often had cause to remark how quick the locals can be to denigrate themselves for the abuses they visit on the Spanish tongue.

'Is she still living in the block there across the street?'

'I imagine so.'

'When did you last see her?'

'Couple of weeks ago.' He shrugged. 'Maybe more.'

'Know anything else about her?'

'Can't say I do, no.'

'But she comes in here?'

'For breakfast sometimes, yeah.' He shot me a sharp sideways glance. 'Why all the questions anyway, if you don't mind me asking?' he said. 'You a cop or something?'

'Just a friend.' I smiled and pocketed the photograph.

The merest suggestion of a twinkle came into the man's eyes, though the rest of his face continued to hang down like washing left out in the rain, and he said, 'She's quite a looker.' Then he turned and went inside the café, to see to my order.

It was a beautiful day and the sun's rays were busy giving the Bocanazo a regular toasting. I wiped a bead of sweat from my nose as I sat and watched the entrance to the block across the street.

The man came back and placed my beer and the ham roll down in front of me. He looked at me. 'She in some kinda trouble?' he asked, his brown eyes narrowing in a suspicious expression.

'No, not that I know of... I'm just looking for her.'

'You're a friend of hers, you said?'

'That's right.'

The man looked like he wasn't sure whether or not to believe me, so I gave him my brightest and most honest Eton smile, and he nodded, still not seeming entirely convinced. I suppose he saw a slim, stylish-looking Englishman, with a caramel tan dressed in an expensive linen suit, and must've wondered what a guy like me was doing come here and asking him all these questions. 'You've forgotten to bring me my olives,' I said.

The man went back inside, then returned moments later with the olives in a small dish. I tasted my beer then had a nibble on an olive, before I started in on the ham roll. I kept my eyes on the entrance to the block across the street as I ate. The cured ham tasted pretty good and the bread was fresh.

At that moment a navy-blue Mercedes came purring round the corner and pulled up outside the block, just along from where I'd parked. Now if you're sitting on the terrace of a café further down in the *pueblo*, then seeing a Merc go by might not seem to be any big deal. But the Bocanazo isn't further down in the *pueblo*, and they don't get that class of automobile up this way very often, to the best of my knowledge. Or if they do, then it's only because the car is on its way somewhere else, to the seafront, or some place where people who aren't broke live. But here was this Merc pulling up right across the street from where I was sitting, just a little way down from my Porsche.

Interesting, I thought, bringing out my iPhone and taking a photo of the driver as he climbed out of his car. I left a five-euro note under my plate and set off. I took a photo of the registration plate of the Merc and another of the car itself, before I followed the man into the block of flats and began to climb the stone steps.

Not wanting to tread on the man's heels, I slowed down and let him get to the top before I began to climb the final flight. I took my time going up and, as I approached the landing, I saw that the man was ringing the bell I'd tried earlier. And he wasn't having any more luck than I'd had, which didn't surprise me. Now I had to invent a pretext for being on the top floor, so I took my wallet out and dropped it in such a way that the contents fell all over the place. That gave me an excuse to hunker down on my haunches and gather up my credit cards and file them all away in my wallet. As I was doing that, the man I was following gave up ringing the bell, and I got a good look at him as he turned. He was five ten, of lean build, short brown hair that he'd greased down and combed back, pale complexion, black pinstriped suit, white shirt and black lace-up shoes. His clothes smelt of money and the good tailoring that comes with it. In order words, the guy looked all wrong for the Bocanazo.

Perhaps he's Gisela Schwartz's boyfriend, I thought. Although he must be pushing forty, so the word hardly seemed to fit. Lover, then. But I was only guessing, of course.

I wondered briefly if I should stop him and ask what his business was with Gisela Schwartz; but I rejected the idea no sooner than it had occurred to me. I gave the man a little slack before I followed him back down the stairs, and he was climbing in behind the wheel of his Merc by the time I got back down to the street.

I ran back to my Porsche, climbed in and set off in pursuit. My task was made easier by the fact that he drove at a leisurely speed up out of the Bocanazo; but then he stepped on it a little, as he headed out of town and up into the hills. It was easy enough to follow him at a discreet distance, without giving the game away at first, but then it got more difficult as the traffic thinned out. And before I could work out whether or not he knew he was being tailed, he drove off the road and headed for an isolated farmhouse.

I drove on past and pulled over in a little copse of trees and killed the engine. Down below the coastline was spread out. It all looked harmless enough down there from this distance. The sort of place made for families to come and enjoy a relaxing holiday. Spend some time on the beach and get a tan. Well, it was that all right, only it was a whole lot of other things, too. They don't call it the Costa del Crime for nothing.

I climbed out of the Porsche, locked it with a swish of the remote, and headed through the pine trees; then the land sloped up towards the farmhouse, where the man I was following must have gone. I spotted his Merc. He'd driven along a dust path for about three hundred metres and pulled to a halt in a little forecourt, and I watched him get out of the car and go into the house. He didn't look around, so I figured he couldn't have seen me.

It was hot and I could feel sweat running down my back as I walked over the dry land towards the house. It didn't seem to be much of a place from the outside. Just a sort of caramel-painted rectangular-shaped box, with two large windows either side of the front door, both covered with black iron bars, and a pitched roof with red tiles. The place had a fair bit of garden, and was fenced off from the dry stony land I was walking on. I went over to the fence and peered in at the property, before I walked along, crouching as I did so, towards the entrance to the driveway where the Merc had entered.

Still crouching, I hurried over to the back of the house, and stepped onto the stone ledge that went round the building. I peered in through the back window but didn't see anything of interest, so I tiptoed along the ledge, then stopped by the side of the next window I came to and stood with my front pressed against the wall and listened. Birds were busy chirruping and a car was driving along the road, then I heard a voice. It was a deep masculine voice but I couldn't make out what it was saying. I peeped in through the window and saw the man I'd been following in profile. He had a telephone pressed to his ear.

Just then, something hard hit me on the back of the head.

4

When I came round, I was lying on the floor and my head hurt. I reached back and felt the big lump I had there. As I did so, I wondered where I was and who had hit me. Whoever it was, they were long gone. Above me there was a high white-painted ceiling with thick wooden beams going across it, and the tiled floor was as hard as a bastard. Then I saw a man sitting on a Laura Ashley-type sofa. The man wasn't looking very chirpy. In fact, he was looking very dead. That wasn't surprising because he'd been shot in the forehead and there was blood everywhere.

I got up and went through the dead man's pockets. I found his wallet and in it was his ID card or *carné de identidad*. I took a close look at it. Juan Ribera was the man's name. I took out notebook and pen and jotted down the man's name and NIE number. There was nothing else of any interest in the man's wallet, so I put it back where I'd found it.

Seeing the telephone in the corner of the room, I called the local police. 'There's a Juan Ribera sitting on the sofa in his living room,' I told the man who'd picked up.

The officer said, 'That's nice for him. Anything we can help him with? Perhaps he'd like some champagne sent over along with a few choice *pinchos*.'

'I doubt he'd be in a state to appreciate it,' I replied. 'But the coroner might when he arrives.'

'I see... in that case, perhaps you'd like to tell me where we can find him?'

I gave the man directions, and he asked who I was. Some people do ask such naïve questions, I find, don't you? I hung up and left the house. Before I got back to my car, I heard the police sirens. Whoever it was that had hit me must have called them. No doubt he planned on framing me for the murder. As it turned out, I'd come round before the cops showed. I figured it must be my lucky day and so I'd better make the best of it.

I hid in a ditch down by the road, and watched the police drive up then climb out of their cars and go into the house. Then I hurried the rest of the way back to my Porsche, climbed in and set off as discreetly as I could.

I drove back to Bardino and parked outside of Las Palmas, the big hotel in the middle of the *pueblo* overlooking the seafront. Upon entering, my senses were immediately stirred by the pressed and starched air of the interior. I made my way over to the reception desk. The man behind it was busy doing something on a computer. Fiddling his income tax, most probably, like any self-respecting Bardinado. If you want to get past a person in Bardino without their noticing you, act like you want to ask them a question or get them to do something. It's a manner I've perfected over the years. Any Bardinado worth his salt can spot it a mile away and, realizing that you want him to perform a duty of some kind, he will instantly begin to act as if you were invisible. Thereby having achieved my aim and conferred on myself a cloak of invisibility, I took the elevator up, then made my way along the carpeted corridor to room 423.

I knocked on the door but there was no sign of life inside, so I took out the lock picks I carry with me wherever I go and made short work of getting the door open. I entered on tiptoe, just in case the occupant was sleeping or in the shower–and saw immediately that there was nobody in the bedroom. I took a quick look in the bathroom, to ascertain that I had the place to myself, before I rummaged through the drawers in one of the bedside cabinets. I found the passport of one Mark Wellington, an ugly pug-faced guy with a sleepy look in his eyes. I went through the drawers in the cabinet on the other side of the bed. There was no passport for any Inge Schwartz. Nothing, in fact, to suggest a woman was staying in the room. A boxing magazine lay on the bed, and there was a faint odour of cigar smoke.

So Inge Schwartz fed me a line in baloney, I thought, and ground my teeth. There'd been something about the woman I hadn't liked right from the first moment I set eyes on her, mixed in with all the stuff about her there was to like. Things that I had to confess, to myself at least, were legion. Question now was, what was the woman's game? And who was she playing it with?

Apart from me, that's to say.

I went out onto the balcony and looked down at the beach. It being the middle of September, the season had more or less finished, but there were people on the beach down below. Not as many as you'd find in July and August, but the sand was seeing some action. Give it another month or so, and the temperature would drop and the tourists would stop coming. The kind of people I was interested in came here all the year round, though, which I guess was bad news for the town; but it provided me with a way to earn enough to eat and drink and do a few other things.

I left the room, took the elevator down and went back to the flat in the Bocanazo. Nobody came to the door when I knocked, so I took out my lock picks and went to work. The door opened directly into the living room, which was a medium-sized affair with a low ceiling. The floor was covered with the sort of linoleum that pretends to be tiles and there was an old cherry-red moquette sofa directly to my right, against the wall. Over by the window, a matching easy chair had been squeezed in between the sofa and the French doors that gave on to the tiny balcony. The flock wallpaper was a sickly, mawkish burgundy, and an old television set was sitting on a sideboard that faced the sofa. Though old, the furniture looked like it would collapse long before it got to become antique; and even if by some miracle of science or fortune it were to last that long, no future antiquarian would ever want to come near it with someone else's barge pole. There was a smell of stale beer and au de cologne in the air, and old copies of *Pronto* and *Elle* were splayed out on a cheap glass-topped coffee table.

I held my .38 out in front of me, just in case there was going to be some action, as I veered to my left along the short narrow hallway. There were four doors leading off it. The door immediately to my right was ajar, and I gave it a gentle nudge. I found myself looking in at a small bathroom. A shower with a curtain rail and a toilet were squeezed in next to each other on the far wall. I pulled the curtain back, to assure myself there was nobody in the shower. There wasn't.

Just then I heard what sounded like a key in the front door, so I turned and let myself into the room across the hallway and found myself in a bedroom. It was a girl's room all right. The bedspread was pink for a start, which I figured was a bit of a giveaway. And there were heart-shaped mirrors with fuchsia-coloured frames. Right now, though, I was more concerned with the fact that I had company. I hid behind the door and, peering through the crack, saw a man dressed in jeans and a red T-shirt. He was about five-eleven, and slim all over except for about the gut. He had blond hair and didn't look Spanish.

Figuring it was time to introduce myself I stepped out from behind the door, and shuffled along the short hallway, keeping my .38 pointed at the man.

He looked at me without appearing to see me at first, and then he saw the .38. 'Hey,' he said, 'what the fuck is this?'

'Who are you?' I asked him.

'Funny question to ask a man when you've broken into his flat.'

'It would be if this really was your flat, only I know that it isn't.' I didn't really *know* this, but I'd figured it was perhaps time to hazard an inspired guess and see where it took me, if anywhere.

'Huh?'

'I'm looking for the girl who lives here, Gisela Schwartz.'

'Why'd you expect me to know where she is?'

'Because you're in her flat.'

'She said she was going away for a time, and asked if I wanted to stay here while she was gone and keep an eye on the place.' His Spanish seemed fluent enough if freighted with a heavy accent. I'd have said he was German or something along those lines. Perhaps he was related to the Schwartz sisters. 'Who are you anyway,' he said, 'her ex or something?'

'No.' I took out my badge and tossed it at him. He caught it and looked at it.

'A private dick.'

'You can read. I'm impressed.'

'One who thinks he's clever.'

'Cleverness is a relative concept,' I observed. 'But let's just say that I'm the one holding the gun.'

'Which makes you right, does it?'

'You'd better believe it, buddy,' I said. 'You still haven't told me your name.'

'It's Kurt.'

'What's your surname? And don't tell me it's Cobain.'

'Heinlich,' he said. 'Look, just take what you want and go, okay?'

'What's your relationship with her?' I asked him.

'You could call me a friend.'

'That what she calls you?'

'Sure hope so,' he said. 'She's let me stay in her flat anyway, so what do you think?'

'I don't think anything.'

'I don't like to have to say it, but it kinda shows.'

'You in the habit of throwing wise cracks around when you're standing in front of a man with a gun?'

'I don't make a habit of it,' he replied. 'But then, guys don't make a habit of breaking into flats I'm staying in and questioning me at gunpoint.'

'I'm very pleased for you.'

'If you were that pleased you might consider lowering your peashooter.'

'Already considered it,' I told him. 'Didn't figure it as a sensible option.'

'It might be a healthier one.'

'For you or me?'

'Both of us.'

'Can't say I follow your logic.'

'The thing might go off,' he said.

'That's what it's made to do.'

'The guy who made it wasn't thinking about the consequences.'

'Sure he was,' I objected. 'He was thinking of how much money he'd be able to make from selling it.'

'Like I say,' the man said, 'he didn't think the consequences through. And neither are you.'

'What consequences would these be, pal?'

'You wouldn't want to kill me.'

'Why wouldn't I?'

'Why would you?'

'You tell me, pal. You're the one with all the ideas.'

5

Of course I had no intention of killing anybody, but even so it was interesting to hear the guy talk and try and work out what he was thinking. Besides, allowing him to blab gave me a little time to consider the situation.

He said, 'You'd do some serious time, for one thing.'

'If they caught me.' I was following the logic of the conversation, no more nor less. Just seeing where it would lead. He was the one who'd brought up the subject of my wanting to kill him, after all. And if he was so keen to insist on finding reasons to be afraid of me, then I couldn't see why I should tell him any different.

'Sure they would,' he said. 'Besides, you don't even know who I am.'

'Yes I do, you're a friend of Gisela Schwartz.'

'That's no reason to kill me, is it?'

'I didn't say it was,' I said. 'Neither did I say I wanted to kill you, but I will if I need to. Now make yourself comfortable.'

He sat on the moquette sofa, but I wouldn't have said he looked at ease on it. Mind you, it didn't look like the kind of sofa anybody would ever be able to get very comfortable on. Then again, it isn't always easy to make yourself feel at home when a stranger's pointing a gun at you.

He dropped his hand onto the cushion to his side.

'Put your hands on your knees, where I can see them.'

'Any reason you wanna see my hands?'

'Maybe I like to look at them.'

'You just like hands in general,' he said, 'or my hands in particular?'

'Quit the wise guy talk and do as I say.'

He did as I said.

'There,' I said, 'I knew you could do it if you tried.'

'Now what?'

'I'm going to ask some questions and you're going to give me answers.'

'I had a feeling you were gonna say something corny like that.'

'I want to know what Gisela Schwartz has got herself mixed up in.'

'I had no idea she'd got herself mixed up in anything.' He shrugged and looked at me with the kind of expression schoolteachers must be used to seeing on the faces of kids who don't follow a word they're talking about. I wondered if this guy was really as ignorant as he pretended, or if he had reasons of his own for playing the class dunce.

'No,' I sneered, 'you're the sort of guy who doesn't know anything, right?'

'I wouldn't go that far.'

'Now you're starting to test my patience,' I said, 'and I wouldn't do that if I were you, seeing as I'm the one who's holding the peashooter. So why don't you quit the clever talk and have another try.'

'Look, if I knew where she was I'd tell you.'

'What was Gisela Schwartz doing in Bardino?'

'She worked at a bar down on the seafront. *Georgie's* is the name of the place.'

'Until when?'

'She packed it in a coupla weeks back.'

'Why?'

He shrugged. 'Gisela's not one to tell people everything about what she does. She's kinda private and proud, y'know?'

'So how's she been supporting herself since then?'

'I guess she has some money saved up, but I mean it's really none of my business.'

'How long have you known her?'

'We first met three or four months ago. We dated and slept together a few times, nothing serious you understand.'

'You know anything about her sister or her family?'

'Nope, nothing at all.' He shook his head. 'She's from Germany, I know that much.'

'Where in Germany?'

'Hamburg... I'm from Munich, which is nowhere near where she's from, but even so our both being German's something we have in common.'

'So what's she into–selling drugs, is it, or what?' I knew I was clutching at straws, but there was nothing else to hand for me to clutch at.

'Gisela's not that kind of girl,' he said.

'So what kind of girl is she?'

'She's nice, beautiful, funny... and law-abiding.'

'That's quite a character reference.'

He shrugged. 'Also happens to be true.' He sighed and said, 'Listen, I don't know what you think she's done, but whatever it is I'm sure you must have your wires crossed somewhere. I was you, I'd leave the girl alone.'

'Thanks for the advice. I'll remember not to take it sometime.'

He frowned. 'Thought you'd say something like that.'

'The name Juan Ribera mean anything to you?'

'No...why, should it?'

'What about Mark Wellington?'

He shook his head. 'Now if you'd said the *Duke of Wellington* it might've been different.'

At that moment I heard a noise from behind me. Whoever it was, they must have come from one of the two rooms I didn't have time to check. Before I could turn, whoever was there said, 'Don't move unless you wanna hole in the back of your head.'

I figured I'd better not move.

'Now drop the gun.'

I dropped it.

As I did so, the German reached under the cushion on the sofa and brought out a gun. He was pretty fast but not fast enough, because he took a shot to the head before he could fire. The force of the bullet threw him back against the sofa, so that he lay there with his arms and legs splayed, dead fish eyes looking up at the ceiling. As this happened, I reached down for my gun. But just as I straightened up and was about to turn, something hard hit me on the side of the head and that was the last thing I knew—for a while, anyway…

6

When I came round, it didn't take me long to realize that I was in the middle of a crime scene. There were uniforms, plainclothes officers and members of the *Policía Científico* team all over the place. The latter were dressed in weird outfits that made them look like astronauts.

Somebody helped me to my feet and said, 'Hey, we got a live one' over his shoulder.

I shook my head and looked into the man's face. He was mid-thirties, wavy short black hair, tanned face, five-nine or ten, slim, dressed in jeans, trainers and a pale-blue shirt that he wore open at the collar. I knew him. His name was Salvador Cobos, and we kind of got along. By which I mean that he tolerated me a little more than some of his colleagues, because I think he knew I was basically an honest guy and that I wanted the same thing he wanted, which was to catch the bad guys, even if I did get in his hair from time to time.

A look of curiosity came into his eyes, bringing the faintest suggestion of a smile along with it. 'Boy, you're lucky you didn't go to the same place as your buddy on the sofa.'

'I know,' I said, 'it doesn't look like much of a sofa, does it?'

'Still making with the wisecracks, huh?' He shook his head. 'You find yourself in the middle of a scene like this and you act like it's a joke?'

I shrugged and said, 'Guess I'm just the sort who always likes to see the jar as being half full instead of half empty.'

'I guess you are at that.' He looked me up and down like he'd just seen me for the first time. 'So perhaps you wouldn't mind telling me what happened here?'

'Still trying to work it out myself.'

'Tell you what,' Cobos said, 'why don't we take you down to the *Jefatura* and give you a push in the right direction?'

'Is there really any need for that, Sal?'

'I think there is, Arthur, yes.' He frowned and appeared to give the matter some further consideration for a moment, before he added: 'I think there most certainly is.'

So they took me down to the station, over by the mosque there, and led me into the Serious Incident room. I was given a black plastic chair to sit on, and Salvador Cobos sat the other side of the gunmetal-grey desk. There were pictures of offenders who were wanted by the police on the wall directly behind Cobos's head. The white walls were bare otherwise. I looked at some of the mug shots and thought what an ugly bunch they were.

'Okay, Arthur,' Salvador Cobos said, 'we can do this the hard way or we can do it the easy way.'

My Spanish is reasonably good, by which I mean that I can understand what the locals mean most of the time, certainly when they're speaking formally. And when they're not, I can usually get the gist. I looked at Sal and weighed the situation up. I only needed a moment to do this, because it was obvious that I didn't have a leg to stand on. 'Look,' I replied, 'why don't I tell you what I can, Sal, and save us both a lot of hassle?'

'I'm listening.'

'There's something going down, but I'm not sure what it is,' I said. 'I was given this address, the one you found me at...a source told me a friend of hers was living there, only she seemed to have disappeared.'

Salvador Cobos lit up a cigarette, took a drag and exhaled out of the corner of his mouth. He screwed up his eyes so that he peered at me out of tiny crevices in a face that was dried sandstone. He offered me the pack, perhaps because he wanted me to share in his suffering. I shook my head. 'I kicked the habit,' I said. 'Get to live longer that way, so they tell me.'

'Interesting logic,' he said.

'Stuff fucks up your lungs, Sal. There's no two ways about it.'

'Since when did they start saying that putting yourself in situations where you're likely to get shot's good for your health?'

'That's different.'

'How come?'

'It's work. I do what I have to do. If I get shot, so be it.' I dug out a smile from somewhere. 'It's happened to me before.'

'You got lucky.'

'Maybe I'll get lucky if it happens again.'

'Maybe you will,' he said. 'Then again, maybe you won't.'

I shrugged. 'I'll take my chances.'

Salvador Cobos shook the caterpillar of ash that had formed on the end of his cigarette into the plastic cup he was using for an ashtray. 'Who gave you the address?'

'My client,' I said.

'Your client got a name?'

'Sure has, only I can't give it to you.'

'*Won't* you mean.'

'You know the way it is, Sal.' I gave him the benefit of my breeziest smile. 'I've got my job to do and you've got yours. If I can help you any way without making it impossible for me to do my work then I will. If not, then… well, that's where I draw the line.'

He sighed. 'Strikes me this line of yours is likely to get you in trouble with the law more often than not.'

'The law is an ass, Sal, you know that.'

'And the man who takes it too seriously's an even bigger one, right?'

'You said it.'

'You're not helping me, Arthur,' Sal Cobos said. 'And that means you're not helping yourself.'

'Like I just told you, I'll help you all I can.'

'Okay, so who's the guy who was shot?'
'He told me his name was Kurt Heinlich.'
'That sounds German.'
'From Munich, or so he told me.'
'You believe him?'
'How should I know?'
'How did you end up in the flat?'
'I let myself in.'
'With a key?'
'No.'
'How then?'
'Without a key.'
'I guessed that much,' Sal Cobos said. 'It's called breaking and entering.'
'Bit harsh.'
'What's harsh about it?'
'I only went there to visit someone who was out,' I said. 'If she'd been home then she might have let me in.'
Sal Cobos took a last pained drag before he killed the cigarette in his makeshift ashtray. 'I'd say you had a pretty weird relationship with the truth, Arthur.'
'Truth is a relative concept,' I said. 'Hadn't you heard?'
'You been reading that Albert Einstein guy again, Art? You wanna be careful, he'll play with your mind, fuck you up big time.'
'How'd you work that out?'
'He only works with theoretical particles that are so small they hardly exist. In fact, for our purposes we can say they *don't* exist.'

'That's impossible.'

'But you know what I mean,' he said. 'We're both in the business of chasing criminals, who are not invisible.'

'That's open to question,' I replied. 'Some of the best criminals stay invisible practically forever.'

'Now you're getting clever on me again, Art.'

'You're the one who brought up Einstein, Sal.'

He sighed. 'I dunno why,' he said, 'but whenever I talk to you it always ends up getting complicated.' He frowned. 'I mean why can't anything ever be simple and straight down the line with you, Arthur, huh?'

'I'm giving it to you simple and straight down the line, Sal… I just told you the guy's name and where he's from.'

'We already know that, Art, and his name wasn't Kurt Heinrich—'

'Hein*lich*,' I corrected him.

'Or Heinlich, either, and he wasn't from Munich.'

'That's news to me.'

Sal Cobos looked me in the eye like he was trying to work out whether I was on the level. I looked right back at him, as levelly as I could.

7

Sal strummed his fingers on the desk and said, 'How did you come by the idea his name was Kurt Heinlich and he was from Munich?'

'He said so himself, like I already told you.'

'When was this?'

'After I entered the flat.'

'You ever see or talk to this guy before?'

'No.'

Cobos gave me another of his straight looks. It was as he were trying to see into my mind. 'Are you on the level, Art?'

'I've no reason not to want to help you on this,' I said. 'Only thing I can't tell you's the name of my client.'

'What's the relationship of your client to the German?'

'Again, I'd help you if I could,' I replied, 'but I really don't know the answer to that yet.' I threw up my hands. 'Sounds like you know more than I do, Sal.' There was a first time for everything, I supposed.

'How did you end up on the floor?'

'Somebody hit me from behind.'

'Who hit you?'

'Didn't see who it was,' I said. 'If I had I'd've stopped him from hitting me.'

Sal Cobos ran a hand through his black hair, which was tinged with grey at the temple. 'Sounds like you've really got yourself mixed up in something this time, Arthur.'

'Sounds like I have.'

We looked at each other some more in silence.

He sighed in a way that let me know just how weary he was with my little act. 'What about Juan Ribera?' he said. 'Run through how you ended up at his place for me again.'

'I was watching the flat in the Bocanazo when a Merc shows, and this guy gets out and enters the block I'm watching. Well, Mercs aren't so common in the Bocanazo, as I expect you know, so I went in after the guy.'

'And?'

'He knocks on the door to the flat I've been told to keep an eye on.'

'You see him do this?'

'That's right,' I said. 'Okay, look I'll give you the full rundown, but then you've got to play fair with me, right?'

Sal nodded. 'Okay.'

'Nobody's home, or if they are they're not opening up, so he goes away and I follow him in my car to a farmhouse up in the hills.'

'Who shot him?'

'Not sure.'

'Somebody hit you again?'

I nodded. 'I was peeping in through the window at him... he was on the phone to somebody, and then something hard hits me on the back of the head... When I come round, I'm lying on the floor inside the house. I sit up and there's the guy I'd been following on the sofa, and he's not looking very alive.'

'So what do you do then?'

'I go through his pockets, find his ID card and learn from it his name's Juan Ribera, then call you guys before I make my exit and drive back over to the Bocanazo.'

'Where you pick the lock to invite yourself into the flat, only to get yourself into another pickle.'

'That's it,' I said. 'Anyway, I've told you everything I can, so what about telling me who the German was and what he and Juan Ribera were up to?'

'We're not sure what they were up to yet, Art, but we do know that they were both involved with organized crime. Ribera was working with a bunch of guys who were mostly Serbs. As for the German, his name was Joaquim Gross and he was with a group of Germans who've been making their presence felt more and more in the criminal underworld of late.'

'It sure sounds like I've got myself in the middle of something.'

'Mm.' Sal Cobos didn't look impressed. 'I oughta lock you up in a cell and forget where I put the key.'

'But you don't want to do that.'

'Don't I?'

'No.'

'What makes you so sure about that?'

'I'm your bait, for one thing,' I said. 'You sling me out into the sea on your hook and things start to happen, right?'

'That sure is true, but it's always things that *shouldn't* happen. Dead bodies have a nasty habit of collecting around you.'

'Exactly...that means I'm close to something.'

'Close to what...?'

'I don't know yet,' I said. 'But neither do you. We both want to find out, though, and so there's a sense in which we're playing for the same team.'

'I wouldn't go that far.'

Neither would I, but I didn't want to tell Cobos that. 'We both want to catch the bad guys, and you know that so long as I'm out there dangling in the water the bad guys are likely to come out of hiding. You're not quite sure why, but that doesn't really matter at this stage.'

'Okay, but whatever team it is you think you're playing for, Art,' Sal Cobos said, 'you'd better shape up and stop scoring own goals, or you'll find yourself sitting on the bench.'

'I've had a run of bad luck lately, Sal.'

'So you'd better start getting some good luck, and quick, Arthur, if you know what's good for you.'

'I'll go and consult my astrologer.'

'Still with the wisecracks, huh?' Cobos shook his head. 'Don't you ever let up?'

'I guess not.' I stood up. 'So I take it I'm free to go, then?'

'For the time being,' he said. 'Go and enjoy your freedom while it lasts, because I have a funny feeling it's not going to be for very long.'

'Been looking in your crystal ball again, Sal?'

'Yeah, only they call it a computer nowadays... I've been checking on the stuff that's accumulated in your file over these past few years, ever since you came down here and started up as a dick, and I have to tell you it makes for some pretty sorry reading.'

'You ought to take a leaf out of my book and read a couple of pages of Jane Austen every night in bed before you sleep,' I said. 'Be likely to have a much more calming effect on your nerves.'

'Jane *who...*?'

I gave him a sort of wave-cum-salute as I went out the door.

8

I'd barely eaten all day and it was coming up to six in the evening, so I went into a bar on Calle Veracruz and took a seat near the window. The waiter came over and I told him I'd have an *ensalada mixta* and the *rabo de toro*, or mixed salad and bull's tail, and I'd have a carafe of Rioja to help it down.

My head was hurting from where I'd been hit, and I was aching from where I'd fallen, and my belly was noisy with hunger, but I began to feel better as I ate. When I'd finished my meal, I had the waiter bring me a *café con leche* with a glass of brandy.

I tasted the coffee and then I tipped the *cognac* into it and stirred to make what the Spanish call a '*carajillo*'. I had just sipped it when my mobile began to ring.

'How are things going?' a female voice asked. It was Inge Schwartz.

'Oh so-so.'

'Have you managed to find my sister yet?'

'No, but I did nearly get killed a couple of times. Where are you?'

'I'm at the hotel.'

I said, 'I'll meet you in my office in an hour's time.'

'Oh I really don't think that's convenient right now.'

'If you want me to continue to try to find your sister you'll be there,' I told her and hung up.

I settled the bill then left the restaurant and walked along to my office. I went over to the window, pulled one of the slats in the venetian blind open a little and gazed down at the street. The sun had gone down by now and the traffic was passing in a steady stream, the cars all with their headlights on. Then I saw her making her way along the pavement. I saw, too, the way the men she passed would stop and stare; not that she seemed to notice. She moved with a sure-footed rhythm, and then, as she entered the building, I heard her heels as she made her way up the steps. Then I saw the door handle turn and Little Miss Butter Wouldn't Melt breezed into the room. 'So glad you could make it,' I said. 'I missed you earlier.'

'Oh?'

'I paid you a visit at your hotel.' I studied her face to see how she'd respond to what I'd just said, but she didn't so much as bat an eyelid so far as I could tell. 'Yes,' I said, 'I went up to your room. It was four-two-three, wasn't it?'

'What?'

'Your room number?'

'Oh, yes.'

'Well I went up but you didn't let me in.'

She shrugged. 'I must've gone out.'

'I didn't say I didn't *go* in,' I said. 'Just that you weren't there to open the door for me.' Her brows bunched and her right one formed a beautiful arch that was almost like a question mark lying on its side. 'Because I did...'

'You did...?'

'Yes.'

'You did what…?'

'Enter your room.'

She took a step towards me and dropped her Kelly bag onto my desk. 'You entered my room?'

'Yes, but you weren't in it.'

'Well that was rather naughty of you, wasn't it, Mister Blakey?'

'I'm apt to do rather naughty things from time to time, Miss Schwartz… I even ate two chocolate sundaes on Saturday.'

'You'll get fat if you're not careful.'

'I worked out afterwards.'

She moved a little closer, so that we were almost touching, then she gave me the old up-from-under look so that her right eyelash cut across her eye. She had the most beautiful blue eyes, and the effect of the eyelash cutting across it made it all the more stunning. She sighed and said, 'Alone?'

'What?'

'Did you work out alone, Mister Blakey?'

'That's kind of a personal question, isn't it?'

'What if it is?' she said. 'Don't you ever get up close and personal with anyone?'

'I have been known to,' I said, 'but I can't see that it's really any business of yours, Miss Schwartz.'

'But I'm your client, Mister Blakey.' She moved closer to me so that her red lips, so full and succulent, were within kissing range and something inside my head did a pirouette. All I'd have to do is lean forward half an inch and—bingo. I held myself still and stiff, only not in the sense you mean, and then I felt my head spin again. It's funny what the proximity of such beauty can do to a man. So much beauty, I thought, gazing on her as an art connoisseur might pore over the Mona Lisa; so much of it, and all of it far too close to home.

'Precisely, Miss Schwartz,' I said. 'You're my client.'

'And do you mean to say that my being so doesn't buy me certain…certain privileges, Mister Blakey?'

'You're being so *what*, Miss Schwartz?'

'My being your client, I mean?'

'Sure it does,' I said.

'What might the privileges I can expect to enjoy as your client be?'

'Complete confidentiality and discretion,' I said, 'and whatever the job is, you can be sure that I always give it my best shot.'

'That's reassuring, I must say… And what special qualifications and experience have you got that make you the man for the job?'

'I've got a badge which says I've the right to work as a private eye,' I said.

'And are you experienced?'

'Yes, very.'

'Would you like to tell me about how you resolved some of your hardest cases?'

I kissed her on the mouth and she didn't do anything to give me the impression she minded it.

9

'Look, Inge,' I said, 'you can stop bullshitting me, okay?'

'I didn't think that's what I was doing.'

'What's the word you use in German, then?' I asked. 'Whatever it is, you weren't in the room at Las Palmas because somebody else was staying in it.'

She smiled so that the corners of her eyes wrinkled up. 'Oh well,' she said, 'you can't expect a girl to tell you everything straight off when she's only just met you, now can you?'

'I expect my clients to play straight with me, Inge, so I can play straight with them.'

'Are you always this hard on your women after you ravish them?' she asked.

'I figured we kinda ravished each other, Inge.'

'Whatever.' She shrugged. 'There's no need to come on so tough, though, is there?'

'There wouldn't be,' I said, 'if I didn't get the feeling I was being taken for a mug.'

She sighed. 'And to think I took you for a romantic.'

'Look, Inge, you're gorgeous, and that's another thing you know very well. What's more, you play on it. So don't take me for an utter fool, okay?'

'I really don't know what you're trying to say.'

'You waft all that beauty and sex appeal you've got around and hypnotize people with it…and you've worked it on me, so I should know, because I'm as big a sucker as anyone when it comes to that sort of thing and I'm the first to admit it.'

'Gee, that was almost sweet and romantic, coming from you. Should I feel as if I'd been complimented?'

'Yes and no.' I leered at her. 'The simple fact is, Inge, that I don't trust you. I could fall for your tricks, and maybe I already have fallen for them, but that doesn't stop me from seeing through it all.'

'Seeing through what, Arthur?'

'You're not being straight with me,' I said. 'In fact, I seriously doubt if you've ever been straight with any man in all your life.'

'That's a rotten thing to say.'

'Maybe it is,' I conceded. 'Only I'm not some kid playing at cops and robbers but a professional private investigator, and I can't have some blonde bombshell walk in here and stomp all over me like I was a piece of carpet. Are we understood?'

'Yes and no,' she said.

'What do you mean by that?'

'I've no idea what makes you think I'm not being straight with you.'

'You act as if butter wouldn't melt in your mouth, Inge, but you're as worldly as a banknote.'

'I'm not sure I like your tone.'

'You weren't meant to,' I replied. 'Because I don't like working for clients who lie to me about where they're staying, and who seduce me in my office afterwards when I question them about it.'

'I thought you were the one that seduced me?'

I shrugged. 'That's just a matter of semantics.'

She sighed. 'Do you mean that you didn't like being seduced?'

'I loved it and you know it, so you can quit the Little Miss Sweet And Innocent act.'

'I don't just give myself to any man like that, Arthur.'

'Maybe you don't,' I said. 'But you do when you want something badly enough.'

'Hasn't it occurred to you that it could've been you that I wanted, Arthur?'

'I'm afraid I'm neither young nor stupid nor vain enough to believe that coming from you, Inge.'

'But why not, Arthur? Don't you believe in love at first sight?'

'Maybe I do,' I said. 'But if so then there's a little voice in my head that tells me I'd be a fool to in your case.'

She dropped her head and made a wonderful job of looking truly hurt. 'You think I'm no better than a common tramp, don't you?'

'That was a beautiful performance,' I said, 'but you really don't need to waste all that effort and talent on somebody like little old me, you know. After all, you have hired me to work for you.'

She slapped me across the face. 'How dare you talk to me like that.'

I felt the blood all rushing to my cheek, where I'd been struck. It was wonderful.

'I'm sorry I hit you.'

'No you're not.'

'Okay, I'm not because you deserved it.'

I smiled. 'There's a real tigress in there under that phony sweet exterior, isn't there?'

She slapped me again, even harder if anything.

'There,' she said. 'That's what you get for talking to me like that.'

I took her in my arms and kissed her on the mouth, and this time she tried to push me away a little at first. I pulled her back close to me and looked her in the eye. She smelled like heaven on a nice summer's day, and her eyes were little blue and black lakes that contained galleons full of untold treasure. She was everything I'd ever wanted and everything I knew was bad for me, all wrapped up in one impossibly attractive package.

'Why do you want to make love to me so much, Arthur, is what I don't understand,' she sighed, 'seeing as you clearly despise me.'

'I despise you and I love you,' I told her honestly. 'You're everything bad and everything good.' I kissed her.

And kept on kissing her for quite some while; then she slipped out of my arms and opened the door. 'I'll call you tomorrow,' she said, and then she was gone.

And I still hadn't even got her to tell me where she was really staying.

10

I wondered for the umpteenth time what it was that Inge Schwartz's sister could have got herself involved in. I blew out my chops like a tired blowfish, then reached into the drawer at the side of my desk and poured myself another large one. I'd just taken a sip of it when the telephone rang. I reached out and picked it up. 'Hello?'

'I hope you're not still angry with me.'

'Look Inge, I need to know what it is your sister has got herself into.'

'But that's what I thought I'm paying you to find out, Arthur.'

'So you're pretty sure she's into something, then?'

'I really don't know,' she said. 'But I'm getting more and more worried all the time.'

'If you were so worried why didn't you go to the police straightaway, before coming to me?'

'I did, but they didn't take it seriously... they seemed to think young women stop writing home all the time, and that it's no big deal. I tried telling them Gisela's not that sort, but they didn't want to know.'

'Two men have already been killed, Inge, and all because of whatever it is your sister's involved in.' I was finding it easier to talk to her on the phone, easier to get my thoughts together, now that I didn't have the solid magic of her beauty there in the room to have to deal with.

'Oh but that surely can't be.'

'I'm afraid it surely can,' I said. 'The names Juan Ribera and Joaquim Gross mean anything to you?'

'No, I can't say they do.'

Somehow I figured she wouldn't have told me if they did.

'Should they?' she asked.

'All I know for sure is that they were both mixed up in the underworld somehow.'

'You mean they were gangsters?'

'That's a fairly grand way of putting it,' I said. 'These two guys were bit-part players, the types that get sent out to do the dirty work. Sure, Ribera drove a Merc and liked to dress like he was big shot. But my hunch is it was all show. He was the sort to spend most of what he had on making himself look the part. My point is, he looked like he was somebody but he wasn't. But he was working for somebody else who was.'

'Was what?'

'Somebody.'

'But what do you make of it all, Arthur?'

'My guess is, Gisela either stepped on the toes of the wrong person, or she had something that they wanted.'

'Something valuable, you mean?'

'Gangsters don't normally do cheap, Inge. It's not their way. It's part of what makes them gangsters.'

'But Bardino seems like such a quiet sleepy little *pueblo* by the sea,' she said. 'Just another holiday resort.'

'It's all that and an awful lot more. And when I say awful, I mean *awful*. They don't call it the Costa del Crime for nothing.'

'Oh poor Gisela...what you're saying is starting to make me more worried than ever.'

'I don't want to frighten you for the hell of it, Inge,' I said. 'But you hired me to find out the truth, and so you may as well know something about the lay of the land down in this part of the world.'

She didn't say anything, and I sat there listening to her breathing down the line at me. A part of me wanted to rush over to wherever the hell she was and fold her in my arms and protect her from all the bad people in the world, and another part of me wondered if she weren't one of the bad people herself. She said, 'So now what are you going to do?'

'I'll take a little stroll down to *Georgie's* later, the bar Gisela was working in, and see if I can turn anything up.'

She said, 'I'm grateful for everything you're doing to help me.'

'No need for that, just so long as you pay me.'

'I don't think you like me a great deal, do you, Arthur?'

'You want to go fishing,' I said, 'go get yourself a rod and take it down to the beach.'

'What on earth do you mean by that?'

'I'll talk to you tomorrow.' I hung up.

I finished what was left in my glass, then locked the office and took a stroll down to the seafront. It was dark by now and there was a pleasant breeze blowing up, and

I could smell the sea as I walked along and hear the rise and fall of the surf.

Georgie's was doing a good trade when I got there. It was a cocktail bar with bamboo tables and chairs outside. Couples were sitting whispering sweet nothings to each other and sipping their drinks, and the place seemed like an advertisement for the good life. For life as a sort of enlargement on the general theme of sun, sea and romance that was what Bardino tried to sell itself as. I walked up a few steps and entered the bar, which was dark with subdued lighting and low-key music. I dropped my elbow on the wooden counter and turned and looked at the couples out on the terrace.

11

The barmaid came over, an attractive girl with fine ash-blonde hair that came down to her shoulders and nice eyes. She was wearing jeans that she must have shoehorned herself into and a white top that didn't do go out of its way to hide her ample cleavage. I told her to give me a Scotch with a glass of iced water on the side.

When the drink came, I handed her a ten-euro note then took a sip of my whisky. It tasted pretty good. I find that Scotch usually does. The barmaid came back with my change, and I took out the photograph Inge Schwartz had given me of her sister and held it up. 'This is Gisela Schwartz,' I said. 'I was told she worked here.'

The girl nodded. 'She doesn't anymore.'

'Any idea why she left or where she went?'

She shrugged and her cleavage shrugged along with her. 'The girl at the table over there might know,' she said. 'She was friendly with her.'

There were a few couples sitting at tables. 'Which girl? Can you point her out for me?'

'The pretty brunette in the corner sitting with the man in the suit.'

I looked over and saw the girl she meant. I recognized the man she was sitting with, too. His name was Vicente Caportorio and he was a player in Bardino's criminal underworld. 'Thanks,' I said. 'What's the girl's name?'

'Rosa.'

I asked the girl if she'd like a drink. 'Sure,' she said. 'Mine's a Bacardi and coke.' She gave me a sideways look. 'You a cop, right?'

'How did you guess?'

She turned and fixed herself a drink, then came back with my change on a little dish. There wasn't much of it so I left it there.

I sipped my Scotch and looked over at the girl in the corner, whose name I now knew was Rosa, and the man she was with, whose name was Vicente Caportorio. Or Vince, as everybody called him. The man looked like a gangster if anyone ever did. He was wearing a blue shark's tooth suit that looked like it was bespoke, along with a light blue shirt and a burgundy tie. He had a deep tan the colour of roasted peanuts, and his jet-black hair was swept back and gelled down. His face was lean and looked like it had been fashioned with a chisel, but it was the eyes that you noticed. They were alive with the glare of a hungry animal. As for the girl, she was gorgeous in a Penthouse-magazine sort of way.

I took my drink and went over to their table, then stood there for a moment and waited for them to look up and notice me. They didn't seem to want to. They were deep in conversation, and they looked like whatever they were talking about must be pretty interesting. The man, Vince, was drinking Scotch on the rocks and the girl what must be a gin and tonic or vodka. I had the impression they were making a point of not noticing me. Well, you don't get to earn a living in my business if you're the sort who gets upset when people are rude. I sipped my Scotch and carried on standing there, until Vince finally looked up at me. 'The fuck do you want?' he said in a gruff voice.

'Just a friendly word with your lady friend here, if you don't mind. I won't take up much of your time.'

'And what if I do mind?'

I took out the photo of Gisela Schwartz minus two or three years and held it out for the girl to look at. 'You knew her, I believe?'

The girl glanced at it and looked away. Vince did the same. Their faces were a pair of closed books: the sort that you wouldn't want to read.

'Name's Gisela Schwartz,' I said. 'I'm told she used to work here.'

The girl shrugged. 'So?'

'I'm looking for her.'

'You a cop?' Vince wanted to know.

'Kind of,' I said and took out my card.

Vince glanced at it and sneered.

I looked at the girl. 'I've been told you were friendly with her, Rosa?'

'You been told wrong, amigo,' Vince answered for the girl.

I put the photograph away, along with my card.

'Okay,' Vince said, 'you've said your piece so now you can beat it.'

'Maybe I don't like your manners.'

'Maybe you ain't supposed to like 'em,' he said. 'Maybe your problem is you're a little slow on the uptake, chum, *me entiende*? A little slow to get the message, *sabes*?'

'Oh I get the message all right, *chum*,' I told him. 'I just don't wanna hear it.'

A nasty smile spread across the man's face, only his eyes weren't smiling. They had murder in them. 'Maybe you wanna come and talk to me outside.'

I said, 'Anyone ever tell you that you use the word *maybe* too much, Vince?'

That set him thinking, or trying to. 'Who told you my name's Vince?'

He smiled again. 'Ah, I know,' he said. 'I saw you talking to the bitch behind the bar.'

'Wasn't her,' I told him. 'Listen,' I said, 'if you think you're so big and tough then sure I'll come outside and talk to you. But let's leave girls out of it, shall we? Only sissies hit girls.'

That must have touched a nerve somewhere, because he sprang up off the banquette like he was a jack-in-the box and there was a spring affixed to the seat of his trousers. Unfortunately for him, though, the table was in his way, so that he had to move round it before he could get to me. That gave me time to skip down off the step that rose to the booth the pair were sitting in, and as he came at me I moved to the side and tripped him. He fell and I grabbed him and spun him around. His arm flailed, sending flying a tray full of drinks that a passing waiter had been carrying. I heard the crash the glasses made as they shattered on the floor. I got him in a sort of bear hug only from behind, with one arm round his neck. He swung his elbow back and got me in the ribs. I'd been hoping he would be all talk, the way some of these types can be. But this guy was a lump of granite with arms and legs attached. I groaned as I felt my ribs crack and must have let go of him for a moment, because the next thing I knew he'd spun round and was facing me. He threw a punch that I saw coming, but only as it was about to break my windpipe. I ducked and got it in the jaw. I reeled back and felt something hard hit my spine about half way up. I realized I'd hit the counter, and I looked up just in time to see him coming at me again. He was a solid rhino made of stone, only he was a hell of a lot uglier than any rhino I'd ever seen and much more violent. The man was one big ball of rage and hate. But maybe that was his weakness. Because he came charging at me just like a rhino, the way a man does when he has no plan of attack. He just wanted to tear me apart, and that was all he had on his mind. I could sense this, the way you can sense things about your opponent when you're in a fight. The man was all violence and no finesse, and as he came lunging at me I feinted and skipped to the side. Then I hooked one of his feet out from under him, and I was able to use the man's own weight and momentum to send him crashing into the counter. Before he could turn I hit him in the kidneys, then I kicked his other foot out from under him and he went reeling backwards, but managed to reach out and break his fall by grabbing onto the table that the girl he was with, Miss Penthouse, was still sitting at. He regained his balance then glared at me, with his head low. He reminded me of a bull, the way it looks before it's about to charge. And I didn't have a cape handy. Or a sword, for that matter.

Then big trouble struck in the form of something hard on the back of my head.

When I came round I was in the back of a car. I had huge lumps of muscle on either side of me, so there was no way I could move or try anything brave. 'What the fuck is this?' I said.

'You'll find out,' Vince replied from the passenger seat in front.

His mutts had obviously shown just at the wrong time, and I presumed they must have carried me out through the back entrance of the bar where they'd have had the car waiting. My only chance was that some onlooker might have thought to make a note of the reg and phoned it in. But it was a long shot at best. Besides, I thought, the registration plate's almost certainly a false one. What these guys did, they stole different cars and swapped the plates round to make it difficult to trace them. If a cop car didn't appear on our tail before we got to wherever it was I was being taken, then I knew I was up the nameless creek and paddles would be in short supply.

I'd like to be able to say that I was too busy thinking of ways to escape to be frightened, but that wouldn't be true. I was afraid all right.

Looking out through the window, I saw that we were now driving up into the hills. 'Look,' I said, 'the fight was between me and you, Vince, so what's the big deal getting your mates involved?'

'You wanna know what's good for you,' Vince replied over his shoulder, 'you'll shut the fuck up.'

'I don't get it. I just wanted to ask your girlfriend a couple of questions and so you abduct me. What is this?'

'I said shut the fuck up.'

I figured there was no point in trying to goad or shame the man into letting me go, because that tactic just wasn't going to work. So I took his advice and gave my chin a rest.

12

We headed on up into the hills, then we turned off the road up a dirt track. The car jumped and bobbled along worse than ever for the best part of a mile and then it pulled up. I was pulled off the back seat by one of the bears that had been guarding me, and found that we had come to a big farmhouse. A warm breeze was blowing, bringing with it the pungent scent of *dama de la noche*, a smell I'd always liked until now. The two bears took an arm each and walked me over the shingle forecourt. Vince rang the bell and somebody came and opened the door.

No sign of the cavalry, I thought. Never is when you need 'em. Forget what you see in the old cowboy flicks.

They took me through the house and out back. I found myself in a big indoor swimming pool, with pitch lighting and no windows. Vince aimed a wink over in my direction and said, 'Not bad, is it?' He made a noise that was somewhere between a snarl and a chuckle. 'And they say crime don't pay.' He jerked his head back, then looked from side to side like he'd just come to this place for the first time and was amazed by what he saw. 'Well I dunno about you, but the evidence on show seems to point to the contrary, wouldn't you say?'

I didn't say anything.

'Cat got your tongue, has it?'

'What do you want from me?' I asked.

'Who are you working for?'

'I can't tell you that.'

'That's the wrong answer,' he said.

'I never divulge the identity of my client to anyone.'

He made a face like he was pretending to be disappointed. 'I'm afraid that was the wrong answer again.'

He turned to the two bears that'd escorted me in here. 'You know what to do, lads,' he said.

The next thing I knew, one of them disappeared through a door in the far wall and a small crane came down from the ceiling, unfolding itself as it did so. The two men held me as Vince tied a rope around my ankles, and then I found myself being hoisted up out of the air. Then I was swinging in an arc as the crane moved, and when I came to rest I was dangling over the pool.

I heard Vince say, 'Thing you gotta understand is, time's money. And I don't have time nor money to waste on scum like you.'

Then he said, 'Take him down,' and I found myself being lowered into the water.

I took a deep breath before my head went under, and held it for as long as I could. When my breath was all gone, I began to thrash around and just when I was about to pass out I felt myself being lifted back up. I panted and writhed like a fish out of water, as I tried to get some breath back into my lungs.

Vince said, 'You having fun?'

I was still trying to catch my breath and so found myself unable to speak.

'So how about telling me who your client is?'

Finding I was finally beginning to be able to breathe normally once more, I considered how to respond. I didn't fancy the idea of pretending to be a fish again, because I'd already learned how bad at it I was; so I said, 'It's Gisela Schwartz's father.'

'Where's he hanging out?'

'He didn't say.'

'Boy, you really must like the water, huh?'

'No, honestly he didn't... he called from somewhere in Badajoz. Said his daughter'd stopped writing home and he wanted me to check on her and make sure she was okay.'

Vince said, 'So you reckoned I had something to do with all this mess and came looking for me, that it?'

'No, I hadn't even begun to think about you or connect you with it in any way.'

'You're lying.'

I shook my head. 'Fact is, your name hadn't cropped up. I went to *Georgie's* because I was told that Gisela worked there and then I saw Rosie, whom I'd learned was friendly with her, so I tried to talk to her. You just happened to be there with her.'

'Nice try,' he said.

'But it's the truth... anyway you've got no reason to kill me, Vince.'

'What makes you think I need you to tell me what I got a reason to do?'

'Look,' I said, 'I take the point. You wanted to teach me a lesson. Fine. But you don't need my blood on your hands. Where's that gonna get you?'

'Where it's gonna get me's that there'd be one less punk like you running around dirtying the pavements in my town.'

'Look, Vince–'

'You say *look* to me once more'n I'll kill you right here and now, you got that?'

'Okay.' It's surprising how sensitive some of these tough guys can be about words, grammar, semantics, stuff like that. 'But think about it, a lot of people saw us fighting.'

'A lot of people see what I tell 'em to see, and they don't see what I tell 'em not to.'

'Maybe so,' I said, 'but not everyone, Vince. There's always one who talks…and Sal Cobos, the Inspector Jefe del Homicidios in Bardino, happens to be a close friend of mine. He gets to hear I've left the scene, he's gonna come knocking on your door.'

'Like I got to worry about punks like Sal Cobos.'

'Thing about men like Sal,' I said, 'he's got a lot of buddies.'

'So do I got a lotta people.'

'Not as many as Sal's got…he's got the whole of the police force. We're talking thousands of men, Vince. You don't need all that heat.' In reality of course what I'd just said was a gross exaggeration, given how stretched police resources were; but concerns as to the veracity or otherwise of what I had to say were the least of my worries.

'Anybody ever tell you that you talk too much?'

'Lots of people.'

The half-amused look had left Vince's face by now. 'I've had enough of all this talk.' He nodded to the other two men and said, 'Put a mask on him and introduce him to Estrella.'

Somebody must have pulled a lever or something somewhere, because I found myself swirling through the air again. When I came to a stop, there was no longer water but the tiled flooring that ran along the side of the pool beneath me. Then somebody slipped an oxygen mask over my face, and something was being attached to my back.

The goon who was busy with the straps said, 'Boy, you really gonna enjoy what you got comin',' and chuckled.

I didn't like the sound of this.

I figured I wasn't supposed to like it, either.

I wondered who in hell Estrella was supposed to be.

Whoever she was, I didn't want to meet her.

But I knew I was going to, whether I wanted to or not.

13

My dear departed father always had the right idea. 'Go into banking, my son,' he told me. 'Avoid working with your hands or doing physical work of any kind,' he always said. 'And avoid making or creating anything of any sort, too, while you're about it. If you want to earn money then you need to work with money,' was another of his tenets. They were like commandments; only he never set them out in stone. He just kept repeating them over and over again. It was all sound advice. Why had I never listened to him? Probably because he was my father, and guys like me never listen to their fathers. Not even when their fathers give them good sound advice. *Especially* when their fathers give them good sound advice. If my dad had given me a copy of *Thus Spake Zarathustra* and told me to travel the world and seek ancient wisdom in its forgotten corners, I would probably have run all the way to Savile Row and bought myself the best pinstripe I could find, or had myself measured up for said garment, and then seen about trying to make a career for myself in the Square Mile. Go figure.

But why was I thinking about all this now? you may wonder. Well, it's funny all the stuff that can pop into your head when you're dangling on the end of a rope and wondering if the time has come for the finale, and a particularly gruesome and anything but grand one at that. Just then, I found myself moving through the air again, and when I stopped I could see water beneath me once more. So it looked as though I was headed for another ducking. I wondered why they'd fitted me with an oxygen mask this time. What was going on? And who was this Estrella? Or more to the point, *what* was she?

I had the feeling that Vince had something nasty in mind. He didn't strike me as the sort of guy who'd ever have any *nice* ideas, after all. Maybe this is going to be it for me, I thought. Maybe this is going to be the end. Well if it was then there didn't seem to be anything I could do about it.

This time when I went under the water, I had oxygen to breathe. Which might sound like good news so far as it went, only it didn't go very far if you catch my drift. You see, looking through the window in my mask, I was able to see that the wall that ran around the edge of the pool was made of thick glass. And there was an enormous and particularly vicious-looking shark on the other side of the partition. And it wasn't just any old sort of enormous and vicious-looking shark, either, but a great white. In order words, the worst sort.

Then my blood froze as a gate in the partition slid open, and I knew it was only a matter of time before the shark came through the opening and joined me in the pool.

So this is Estrella, I thought.

That bastard Vince wanted to send me on a blind date with a great white shark.

14

I had an affair—no that's too serious a word—an *adventure*, shall we say, with an Estrella once. She'd been no beauty, but she was a nice enough sort of kid. Nothing like *this* Estrella at all.

I just hoped that it would be fast when it happened, and that I wouldn't know too much about it.

Time dragged like a bastard and a bitch combined. I mean you can imagine. Or maybe you can't. Maybe you don't even want to try. I can't say I blame you.

After a while of this, I started to think maybe the shark wasn't interested in me. Maybe it wasn't going to bother to come through the gap in the partition. Maybe it wasn't a very sociable shark. Maybe it was the shy type. Maybe it had already eaten its dinner. Maybe any damn thing, just so long as it stayed where it was. Just so long as *I* didn't end up as its dinner.

Then she made her appearance. She looked almost casual at first, like she wasn't in any particular hurry to come over and check me out. Then she turned and eyeballed me. Estrella. Which means *star* in Spanish. Now there's nothing quite like being eyeball to eyeball with a great white shark, I can tell you. Especially when you're unarmed and dangling underwater from a piece of rope.

Then she made her move and started to come towards me. Now I'd found myself in some tight squeezes before.

They went with the job, you might say. But this one was as bad as any I could remember. Not only that, but I was convinced this squeeze was going to be my last, and just when I feared I was about to become Estrella's dinner, I found myself being hoisted up out of the water at quite a rate of knots. Estrella was within sniffing distance before I left the water, and she jumped up and took a snap at me with her enormous jaws - and only just missed.

I went swirling through the air again, until I was no longer hanging over the water in the pool but the tiles that ran along its edge. Vince and his two stooges seemed to have found the little scene rather entertaining, because they were laughing fit to bust.

Vince said, 'Have fun in there with Estrella, did you?'

'I'm afraid she's not my type…rather too toothy.'

'No, well one man's meat, I guess…although it's not what you think of Estrella that's important, but what *she* thinks of *you*. Whether she finds you to her taste, if you catch my drift.'

The two mutts laughed like Vince was some genius comedian. I reckoned it was easy to come across like a wiseguy when you were in his position. He should try coming out with the comic lines when he finds himself in the situation I was in. 'So anyway,' Vince said, 'you were saying…'

'Was I?'

'About your client, I mean.'

'What about him?'

'It was the dad of this girl's gone missing, you say?'

'Yeah.'

'You do realize you're going to spend some more time with Estrella if I don't believe you?'

'I rather gathered as much.'

'You rather gathered as much, didya?'

'Yeah.'

'What made you gather so much?'

'Look,' I said, 'I have no idea why you're getting so worked up all about nothing. And I've no idea why you got so tough back in the bar either and wanted to fight, just because I wanted to ask your girlfriend a few questions about a girl who seems to have gone missing. And I've no idea why you're torturing me with a shark now.'

'And that's your final story, is it?'

'It happens to be the truth,' I said. 'Unless you'd prefer it if I made up a lot of lies.'

Vince looked at me and there was a twinkle of amusement in his eye 'You know, punk,' he said, 'it's lucky that you came to see me like this because you're just the person I needed to talk to.' He chuckled. 'It's like you were brought to me by Providence, you know that?'

I didn't have the faintest idea what in hell's name he was talking about, so I kept mum and listened to what he was going to say next, figuring he might explain himself a little better.

'I've been hearing about the Rembrandt the sister has and I figured it was time I looked into it a little... and now here you are to tell me.'

'Tell you what?'

'Where she's keeping the Rembrandt, of course, you dumb punk. I gotta spell it out for you?'

'What Rembrandt?' I said. 'I don't know anything about any Rembrandt.'

'Well I guess it's just not your lucky day in that case.'

'If you're gonna kill me,' I said, 'then can't you just shoot me in the head like any other gangster? I mean what's all this shit with the shark?'

Vince looked at me stony-faced, and I had the feeling that he was trying to make up his mind what to do with me. He lifted his chin and moved it around a little, so that the chords in his throat showed. Then he ran a hand through his short black hair. I noticed that he was wearing cufflinks with the figure of a miniature shark mounted on them. The man seemed to have sharks on the brain. 'Look,' he said, 'I know you're lying, okay? I know your client's the girl's sister, so you can quit bullshitting me.'

'It's Gisela's father.'

'The old man's dead,' Vince snapped. 'Now I'm going to say this once and only once. Where's the Rembrandt?'

'This is the first I've heard anything about any Rembrandt.'

'Okay,' he said to the two mutts, 'get him down from there'n drive him some place.'

'Then what, boss?'

I didn't hear Vince's reply, because the next thing I knew I hit the ground and passed out.

15

When I came round, I was in the boot of a car. The road must've been rocky, because I was being shaken about like a lone pea in a can that was being rattled by a playful gorilla. I wondered where I was being taken, and what would happen when we got there. My wrists were tied behind my back and they were hurting like a bastard.

A little earlier, back when I was in the pool with Estrella, I would have settled for a bullet in the head rather than ending up in the shark's belly. But it's funny how quickly a man's ideas on such matters can change. I worked out a theory on that once. Forgotten most of it now. But it had something to do with circumstances. That was it. The relationship between circumstances and a person's attitude. Change the one and you could find the other changing with it. Some philosopher me. Anyway, taking a bullet in the head no longer seemed like such an attractive option.

The car pulled up and I heard doors opening and being slammed shut. Footsteps over dry land. Then a key in the lock on the boot. The lid opened, and the two mutts were standing there looking down at me. Bastards thought they were somebody, because I had my hands tied. They got me up out of the boot, and I found myself looking down over the edge of a ravine. I could just make out the bottom by the light of the moon. It was a long way down. I figured I'd better try and make a run for it.

Only that was easier said than done, with my hands tied behind my back and the mutts holding me by the arms.

The bigger of the two mutts took out a gun. So this was going to be the end. At least that was what they had in mind. But I had a different script up my sleeve. I'd been in tight squeezes before and wriggled out of them, I told myself, so why couldn't I do it again this time? Granted this latest squeeze was pretty tight, but some of the others had been, too, and I'd managed to live to tell the tale. I thought about trying to kick the gun out of the mutt's hand with a karate kick, but he was just out of range. So I took a step towards him. Seeing me do this, he told me to stay put or he'd shoot.

'The fuck you wanna shoot me for?'

'That's none of your business.'

'That's a new one,' I said. 'Since when hasn't it been a man's business if another man shoots him?'

'Never.'

'I don't follow you.'

'You ain't supposed to.'

The second mutt took his gun out, which I took to be a bad sign. My plan to kick the gun out of the hand of the mutt who was aiming at me, and then take my chances with the pair of them went up in smoke on the instant. Not that it had ever been much of a plan. Truth is, I wouldn't have stood a chance. Even I could see that, now that I'd had a moment or two to reflect on it; and I'm a natural born optimist.

The second mutt was aiming at me now, too. 'The fuck're we standing here talking to the bastard for? Let's do him.'

Just then, a car came round the corner in the road, and the beams of its headlights raked us over. The two mutts lowered their guns. They didn't want a witness after all.

It's now or never, I thought, and I turned and went over the side of the ravine. Next thing I know, the world's going ass over tit, if you will excuse the expression, and I'm going down the ravine at a rate of knots. I heard a shot being fired, then a second one, but they both missed. Then I hit something hard and stayed where I was. The impact of the crash took the wind out of me for a moment, and I heard myself let out a groan. It took me a few moments to get my breath, then I looked back up the ravine. I'd fallen a fair old way, and had hit the trunk of an olive tree.

I could see the two mutts up above, peering down over the edge. With any luck, they'd get back in their car and leave.

'You see the bastard?' said one.

'Na...too dark.'

'I can see a lot of the way down and there ain't no sign of 'im, so he must've gone right to the bottom.'

'Guess so...think we should go'n check?'

'No need. I'm sure I got him when I fired.'

'Think I did, too,' the second mutt said. 'But even so, maybe we oughta go'n make sure.'

'Fuck it,' the other mutt said. 'I bought this suit new last week. Last thing I want's to go on a fuckin' climbin' expedition and ruin it.'

'Fucking steep, too.'

'You ain't fucking kiddin' me. Cost me best part of four hundred euros.'

'No, down there, I mean.'

'Oh, yeah.'

'We could fall ourselves if we was to try'n go down there, I meant.'

'Specially in the dark.'

'So we're gonna leave him, then?'

'Fucker's dead, ain't he?'

'I guess he must be.'

''Course he's fucking dead. If you got him with your shot and I got him too then the bastard's gotta be, right?'

'I guess so.'

'Can you stop giving me that you guess so shit, Arturo?'

'What you talkin' about, Juan?'

'You talkin' like you ain't sure.'

'I just wanna be thorough, tha's all. No need to get fuckin' pissy, is there?'

'I understand you wanna be thorough, Arturo, but fuck it, the man's dead, ain't he?'

The mutt called Arturo didn't muster an answer.

'Well fucking ain't he?'

'I guess he is, Juan. Yeah.'

'There you go again, see.'

'See what...?'

'Givin' me that fuckin' *you guess* so shit. What are you saying, Arturo? Are you saying you wanna go down there'n look for the bastard?'

Arturo didn't say anything.

'Well are you...?'

'I dunno, Juan.'

'Well it's about fuckin' time you did know, Arturo... Now what's it gonna fuckin' be? Either we go down there or we don't. Which is it?'

'You already said you don't wanna go down there.'

'I didn't say that exactly.'

'What did you say then?'

'I said the bastard's dead, ain't he? And you agreed with me. Or d'you wanna go down there?'

'No.'

'Why not?'

'Why not what, Juan?'

'Why don't you wanna go down there?'

'Wouldn't wanna have you ruin your new suit, Juan.'

'Fuck my suit, Arturo. Forget I ever mentioned it, you got that?'

'I've forgotten it, Juan.'

'Now d'you wanna go down there, yes or no?'

'I guess not, Juan.'

'You guess not, or you're sure not?'

'Fuck it, he's dead, ain't he? I mean he's gotta be, right?'

'I think so.'

'Let's get the fuck outa here.'

16

Moments later I heard the doors of the car slamming shut, first one then the other. The engine started up with a mechanical purr, and I saw the raking beams of the headlights and heard the wheels biting on the dry rubble up above as the car turned around. Then I heard it set off.

So they were gone. I breathed a sigh of relief and figured it was safe for me to move. My chest felt like it had been in a meat-grinder when I set about disentangling myself from the olive tree that had broken my fall, and it was with some difficulty that I managed to get up onto my knees.

I needed to free my hands, so I knelt with my back to the olive tree and began to rub the rope against the bark. It took me a while but I eventually cut through it. Now I had the use of my hands back, I was in a position to plan how I was going to get out of the spot I was in.

The ravine was too steep for me to be able to climb back up it, and the drop down to the bottom was no better. But a little way below me a natural shelf had formed in the limestone. I eased myself down onto it, and began to walk along. It was dark by now and so I moved slowly, taking care about where I placed my feet. I could see well enough where I was about to step, thanks to the light from the stars, although I had little idea of what lay more than ten or fifteen metres ahead of me. I considered using the torch in my iPhone, but decided against the idea. Perhaps the two mutts hadn't gone very far. What if they'd doubled back, in order to look for me? Or maybe they'd only pretended to drive away, in the hope that I would do something that would enable them to spot me. Like turn on my torch, for instance.

Just then, a car went by up on the road, the beams of its headlights raking through the darkness and temporarily lighting up parts of the ravine before me. Up ahead I could see a bend in the road, so I made my way towards it.

When I rounded the corner, the gradient became even steeper so that I found myself shuffling along a narrow shelf in what was otherwise practically a sheer drop down to the bottom. I've never liked heights, and I could feel the hairs standing up on the back of my neck. Easy, kid, I thought. Slip up here and you can say goodbye to your enemies forever.

I stopped and wondered about whether to turn back. Then another car went past up on the road, and I was able to make out, in the beams of its headlights, the rough contours of the land ahead of me. Some fifty metres or so further along, the gradient changed into a much gentler slope down to the bottom. If I could make it along that far then maybe I'd be able to walk through the ravine and it would lead out somewhere. I reckoned it was worth a try, anyway.

So I pressed on, and as I did so I began to feel rather more hopeful so far as my chances of getting back to safety were concerned; that is, I did until the ledge I'd been walking along all but disappeared. Fortunately, I just managed to see where it narrowed in time: another step and I would have found myself walking on thin air–all the way to the bottom of the ravine. I took a deep breath as I stood there on the last bit of the ledge.

I got down on my knees then reached out a hand and felt the ground ahead of me. Where it continued, the shelf could have been no more than ten centimeters wide. It was far too narrow to walk along. My being unable to see ahead in the darkness further complicated matters. I thought of the torch in my mobile and figured it was safe to use it now. The two mutts would hardly have stayed up on the road this long, on the off chance that I might reveal myself, would they? No, they were too stupid for that, I thought.

When I shone it on the ground ahead of me, I could see in the light of the torch the way the narrow ledge continued, before it broadened out again; and then the sheer drop softened into a gentle slope. If I could only make it along that narrow shelf for another twenty metres then I'd be able to work my way down to the bottom without any risk. But the shelf where it continued was too narrow for me to walk along it. The only way of passing it would be to shuffle along sideways, clinging on to any cracks and crevices in the rock face with my fingertips as I did so. It was an operation that called for an experienced climber; and I suspected that no such climber would attempt the crossing without a safety harness. Only a madman would consider it otherwise, I felt sure. The ledge was so narrow and the rock face at this point was a sheer cliff face. Now it may be fair to say that I've been known to have my reckless moments and, as any private investigator is only too well aware, the job comes with certain risks attached, but I was no climber. In fact, as I may already have mentioned, I do not like heights.

Just then, as I tried to weigh the situation up, I heard voices up above and I turned the torch off. 'So where's the fucking body, then?' said a voice that I recognized: it was Vince, the gangster who had entertained me at his country house a short time ago.

17

'He went down just here somewhere,' said one of the mutts.

By now I had climbed to my feet and pressed myself against the rock face, in the hope of making myself invisible to those above. I just hoped that they hadn't seen the light from my torch.

'Where exac'ly?'

'Just down there it was,' said the mutt. 'We shot him, too, like I was saying, both of us. Ain't no way he coulda survived, Boss. Is there Juan?'

'Na,' said the second mutt. 'No fuckin way, Boss. Man's a goner.'

There was the answer to the question I'd just asked myself: no, they clearly hadn't seen the light from the torch.

'What I don't like,' Vince said, 'is that you ain't really sure, are you, either of you? It just ain't professional, the way you carry on like this... First you shoulda shot the man *then* you throw 'im over the edge, right? Then there's none of this guessin' lark, is there? I mean, there's no need for it, then, if you do it right, is there?'

'No, but we did it right, Boss,' said the first mutt–who must be the bigger one, I thought. The one in the new suit. 'That right, Arturo?'

'Tha's right, Juan.'

So the first one—Fatty in the suit—was Juan, I thought. Juan and Arturo.

'I don't believe this,' Vince said and he shat in the milk.

'Believe what, Boss?'

'You two...must think I'm fucking stupid the pair a you. That what it is, Juan? Think old Vince's gone soft up top, do ya?'

'No, Boss, nothin' like that. Not at all.'

'What about you, Arturo? Thinkin' you can get together with Juan and pull me by the hair is it, or what?'

'No, Vince, course not.'

'What it fucking sounds like to me, I have to say.'

'But he's dead, Boss.'

'Listen to me,' Vince said. 'I'm running things, okay?'

'I know that Vince.'

'Don't call me Vince. It's 'Boss' to you.'

'Sorry, Boss...but what I was gonna say is, the bastard's dead.'

'Already heard you say that, Arturo, and I didn't like it any better the first time you said it.'

Juan said, 'So now what, then?'

'I'll tell you what,' Vince said. 'You two're gonna go down there'n get him and bring him to me.'

'But he's dead.'

'So bring 'im to me like that then.'

'You want the body?'

'I want the body.'

'But it's a sheer drop down there, Boss.'

'Shoulda thought of that before, shouldn't you?'

The one who was called Juan said, 'Can't see fuck all down there in the dark's the problem, i'n'it?'

'Let's shed a little light on the problem, then. Juan. Here's the car keys. Open her up and shine the lights over the side here.'

'Right, Boss.'

Figuring that they would spot me once the headlights came on, I bit the bullet and stepped onto the ledge. It was so narrow that my heels were hanging over the side. Fortune did favour me with a number of handily placed nooks and crannies in the rock face, though, and I was able to prevent myself from falling backwards to my death by gripping onto them with my fingertips. My heart was beating like a lunatic, but there was no time to think: I had to cross the ledge and start to make my getaway before they saw me. To remain where I was just wasn't an option.

I began to shuffle my way across the narrow shelf of rock, and I had managed to get about half way when my right foot slipped and I would surely have fallen to my death had it not been for the strength of my fingers, which gripped the holds I had found in the rock with great tenacity. And as I did so, I was able to find my footing once more. Just then, the car's headlights came on, the long raking beams lighting up a section of the ravine just a few metres to my left.

'The fuck is he, then?' I heard Vince say. 'I can't see the bastard, can you?'

'No, Boss. Maybe he's further over that way.'

Vince shat in the milk again and said, 'Shoulda let the shark eat him.'

'What I thought you was gonna do, Boss.'

'Considered it, only then I thought they can catch you like that,' Vince replied. 'Happened to someone I know. Opened up the belly of his pet croc, didn't they, and there was the evidence lying inside. Better to get rid of it altogether, I thought.'

I felt certain that they would spot me any moment. And once they saw me, there'd be nothing to prevent them from being able to pick me off. I would be an easy target for them, a sitting duck. I had to get across the ledge.

I slid my right foot along a few inches, then freed my left hand and gripped a hold that I had already found in the rock moments earlier. Sweat was pouring down my neck and back, even though the night air was little more than mildly warm. As I moved my right hand I accidentally dislodged a small stone that went skittering down the cliff face. Then I heard a voice–Vince's–say, 'What was that?'

'What?'

'I heard something.' Vince said. Then he called out: 'Move the car so the lights are shining over here.'

The engine let out a growl, and then I heard the tires bite into the gritty surface of the roadside. I feared that the headlights were going to pick me out any moment, and that I was about to get to play pigeon in a pigeon shoot. Then as the lights came raking over the area near to where I was, I saw a big whole or cavern in the rock face just above me. Using the holds that I found in the limestone, I climbed up to the cavern and crawled into it. The next moment the car's headlights came raking over the ledge I had just left. I had just managed to climb up in time. A second later and it would have been too late. I would have been a dead man. But luck had been with me. I was safe–for the time being, anyway.

The roof of the cavern was too low for me to be able to stand, so I crawled along on my hands and knees. Maybe it will lead out somewhere, I thought. Wishful thinking, perhaps; but nothing ventured, nothing gained. I took out my iPhone and turned on the torch so I could see ahead of me. But even with the light from the torch it was still difficult to see whether the tunnel led anywhere, and I figured the only way to find out was to keep on moving.

After I had been crawling in this way for some while the tunnel came to an end, and I found myself looking down over a sort of underground pond, which must have been five or six metres in diameter. On the other side, I could see another tunnel that led upwards. Maybe it would lead up to the road, I thought. At any rate, it was worth taking a look.

Leaving the torch on, I tossed my iPhone through the air and heard it hit rock. Fortunately it hadn't been broken by the impact and, since I had thrown it so that it would be facing me when it landed, I was able to see the water down below. I jumped down into it, and discovered as I did so that it was way too deep to stand in, so I swam the short distance over to the far side; then I dragged myself up onto the bank. I retrieved my iPhone and then began to make my way along the tunnel.

I hadn't gone far before I heard a noise and looked down, shining my torch in time to see a tiny lizard go skittering across my path. I was soaking wet and dog tired, and two or three of my ribs were almost certainly broken, but I was driven on by my will to live and by the desire to get even with Vince and his two mutts. If I were to drop now then they would have won, and I told myself once more that I would see myself in hell before I allowed that to happen.

The tunnel sloped upwards, and this gave me cause to hope that I was heading back towards the road or somewhere near it. I walked about a hundred metres or so, and then my heart did a somersault in my chest as I found myself looking up at the crescent moon. I turned my torch off and pocketed my iPhone; then it was just a case of climbing a wall of rock before I dragged myself out onto what turned out to be a grassy knoll. This last feat of gymnastics proved agonizing, given the state of my ribs; but I was greatly relieved to find myself back on terra firma. And turning my head, I found myself looking down on a parked Mercedes.

Realizing that this must be the car Vince and his two mutts had come here in, I feared for a moment that they might spot me. But fortune favoured me once again, because there was no sign of the three men. Then I heard voices, and realized that they were looking for me down below and that they'd left the headlights of the Mercedes on to help them in their search.

Crouching and moving cautiously at first, I dashed down to the road. From there, I could see that Vince and his mutts had gone along to the part of the ravine where the gradient was gentle enough to make it safe to walk to the bottom, and they were descending the incline.

Figuring they were best left to continue their futile search alone I set off towards the Merc, and I heard the engine running well before I reached the vehicle. The fat man had obviously left it running when he'd turned the lights on, in order to avoid running the battery down. That being so, I figured the key must be still in the ignition, in which case the door couldn't be locked. I tried it and it opened, so I climbed in behind the wheel. Thanks, buddy, I thought, and turned the key in the ignition. The engine growled nicely. I slipped her in gear then brought up the clutch and I was away.

The three mutts down below must have known what had happened straightaway, of course, as soon as the headlights stopped shining over the area of the ravine they were in the process of descending. But it would take them a few minutes to get back up to the road; and when they got there, they'd find themselves short of a car. 'Hard luck fellas,' I said aloud, as I put my foot down.

18

When I got back to Bardino I dumped the Merc by the train station. A glance at my Swatch told me it was ten past three a.m. It had been quite a night. My ribs were hurting like a bastard as I set off for my flat on foot and I was soaked to the skin, but I was still alive and that was the important thing.

The street was quiet and my footsteps echoed as I approached the door to the building; then, as I took the key out of my pocket and slipped it in the lock, I saw in the glass door the reflection of a car pulling up at the curb behind me.

I kept a close eye on the reflection of the car as I turned the key, then I went inside. Perhaps I'm being a little paranoid, I thought, but I'd already been taken for a mug once that night, and I wasn't in any hurry to be caught out again. So, figuring it was better to be safe than sorry, I crossed the tiled lobby and, instead of going up the stairs to my flat, I left the building by the back entrance. Then I doubled back and, peering round the corner, I saw the car still there only now the driver was getting out. I watched him go over to the front entrance to the building. If Vince had sent him—he would only have needed to call one of his boys on his mobile, after all—then he would try and pick the lock, I figured. But he didn't. Instead he studied the names on the console at the side of the door, then he pushed a buzzer. I waited to see what happened. Nothing did. Either the person he was calling on wasn't in, or they weren't in a mood to talk. Few people would be at this late hour. Maybe the man's wife has locked him out, I thought. Only I didn't recognize his face, and I'd seen enough of it in profile by now, courtesy of the light from the streetlamps, for me to do so if he lived in the building. So perhaps the man was calling on his girlfriend, then, I thought. Whoever it was, the other party wasn't interested. It hadn't failed to occur to me that the other party might well be yours truly.

Moving quickly but taking care to be as quiet as possible, I set off and came up behind the man. I wasn't carrying and there was always the chance he might be—in fact, he certainly would be if it was Vince that had sent him over—so I figured it would only be sensible to take every precaution. I gave him the old stiff finger in the back and said, 'Better not move, pal. It's loaded.'

'Don't shoot,' he said, sounding terrified.

'Tell you what, pal, we're gonna play a little game. You tell me who sent you over here and who you've come to see and why, and if it sounds kosher you get to carry on breathing. How's that sound?'

'I'm a journalist,' he said. 'I work for *La Vanguardia*.'

'Likely story.' I knew the newspaper he claimed to be working for had its offices in Figarillo and served the region of Catalonia. That was the best part of a ten-hour drive away.

'No, it's true, honestly... but what's with the gun?'

'What's your name and who are you calling on?'

'Javier Fontana's the name, and I've come here to speak to a man by the name of Arthur Blakey. Works as a private investigator.'

'Funny time to be calling on him.'

'It's kinda important.'

I hooked a foot round the man's ankle and shoved him in the back. He tripped, so that he fell against the glass door, using his hands to break his fall. As he did so, I kicked his other foot out from under him and he bit the concrete. I didn't want to take any chances about him getting up again, so I kicked him in the jaw. And scored with a knockout.

That gave me the chance to go through the pockets of the light grey suit he was wearing. I didn't find a gun, but I did find the man's press card. So he really was a journalist. And his name really was Javier Fontana. Seems it's not only my line of work that comes with certain risks attached, I thought, as I slapped the guy about the chops to try and bring him round.

Then his eyes opened. 'Where am I?' he wanted to know.

'You've taken a trip down south, pal,' I told him. 'You're in sunny Bardino.'

'Oh yeah…' That seemed to register with him. 'And who are you?'

'Name's Arthur Blakey—Art to my friends.'

'Rings a bell.' He felt his jaw where I'd kicked it. 'Ouch.'

'In a little pain, huh?'

'Feel like I've been trampled by a giant rhino,' he moaned. 'Think my jaw might be broken.'

'You took quite a tumble, mister.'

'What happened, exactly?'

'You slipped.'

'No, I didn't.' It was coming back to him now all right, and his eyes flashed with anger. 'You held a gun in my back and then you hit me.'

'Sorry, didn't mean to.'

'How can you attack someone by mistake?'

'Thought you were someone else.'

'But I told you who I was.'

'Sure you did,' I said. 'Only I didn't believe you.'

'Kinda suspicious, aren't you?'

'You would be if you'd been in my shoes a little earlier.'

I could see I'd got his interest now. 'Why, what happened to you?' he asked.

'More a question of what *didn't* happen.'

'Okay, what didn't happen, then?'

'I didn't get fed to a shark in some mutt's swimming pool by a whisker,' I said. 'And I didn't get shot in the head and then have my dead body thrown down a ravine, either. Just missed out on all that by the skin of my teeth.' I considered the statement I'd just made and then decided I ought to qualify it a little. 'Actually I only missed out on the first two of the pleasures I just described.'

'Huh?'

'I took a tumble down a ravine,' I explained, 'only I just managed to avoid getting shot first.'

'I still don't follow.'

'Never mind, it's a long story,' I said. 'Let's just say I had my suspicions that someone who doesn't like me sent you here.'

'This would be the guy who didn't feed you to the shark in his swimming pool, I take it?'

'It would.'

'And would it also be the guy who nearly shot you and threw your dead body over a ravine?'

'That was the two goons he has working for him,' I said. 'But you get the picture… I can see you learn fast. You should go to night school. No saying how far a bright young man like you might go.'

'Who's the guy who wants you dead?'

'One Vicente Caportorio,' I said. 'If you've never heard of him he's a gangster with something of a rep down in this part of the world, and it's a rep he's earned by being a thoroughly vicious savage.'

'I get the picture.' He winced and touched his jaw where it hurt.

'Sorry I hit you so hard.'

'I guess you had a reason.' There was a thoughtful expression on the man's face as he turned his head and looked at me. 'So what did you do to get up this Vince guy's nose?'

'I tried to ask his girlfriend a few questions.'

'Obviously not a man who thinks it's good to talk.'

'You have a nice line in humour, my friend,' I said. 'Carry on like that and you might end up as a private investigator.'

'Since when did private investigators need to have a nice line in humour?'

'Didn't you ever read those Philip Marlowe novels?'

'Never got into Chandler, I'm afraid,' he said. 'Faulkner's more my bag.'

'It's gone three in the morning and here we are talking literature,' I said. 'How about I invite you in for a coffee?'

'Sounds like an improvement on a blow to the back of the head.'

I opened the door and pressed the timer delay light switch, then made my way up the stairs. I kept my eyes peeled while I was about it, just in case, but I didn't run into anybody on the way up who was waiting to give me a nasty reception. And a quick check round the flat, once we'd got in, didn't reveal any of Vince's mutts, either.

'Nobody waiting in the bathroom or behind the bedroom door with a gun, then?' Fortuna said. 'That's a relief.'

'Sure is,' I said, 'although it's always possible they just haven't shown yet.' I went over and double-bolted the front door. 'Things are looking up,' I said. 'Now if only I wasn't out of coffee…' I looked at the hack and saw that he was still feeling jaw on his head where I'd hit him. 'It was coffee you said you wanted, right?'

'Only if you haven't got anything better.'

'What's your idea of better?'

'Scotch, if you have any.'

'You're right,' I said, 'Scotch would definitely be better.' It usually is, I find. 'Won't be a minute.' I went into the bedroom and found some clean underwear and a tracksuit and changed into them, before I returned to the living room and began to search for the Scotch. I found the bottle in the drinks cabinet over by the wall, but to my dismay it was empty. I was still feeling bad about having roughed the man up, and wanted to make amends by giving him the drink he'd asked for. Then I remembered I'd gone to buy some more and left the fresh bottles in the larder. 'Hang on a second,' I said.

When I returned with the bottle and two tumblers, moments later, I saw that my guest had fallen asleep on the sofa. I wondered for a moment whether I should wake him and tell him I had his Scotch, but then figured it would probably be best to leave the man in peace and let him stop the night where he was. It was the least I could do after the way I'd roughed him up earlier. So I set the tumblers down on the table, along with the bottle, and poured myself a stiff one, then I slumped into the easy chair and took pecks at the Scottish treasure while I watched Fontana get his beauty sleep. If he could write half as well as he could snore then I reckoned he ought to be up for a Pulitzer. I knocked back what was left in my glass and got up to give myself a refill. I was feeling a little sorry for myself and tetchy and like Scotch might just have the answer to my problems. I'd been in this sort of mood before many a time, and somewhere there were the empty bottles to prove it.

I struggled up out of the chair, with all the inelegance of a man who's been dangled on a rope as shark bait and thrown down a ravine; a man whose ribs were probably broken and who should really go to see a doctor about it. I figured the doc could wait until the morning. I went into the bedroom and worked off my shoes. They were lace ups and so I had to sit on the bed to do it, and it proved to be a tricky task. Shoeless, I lost the rest of my things and climbed gingerly between the sheets. It was agony lying on my right side, so I figured I'd better turn over. I did it in the end, but it was painful and felt like one of those operations that involve cantilevers and cranes and lots of cables. Okay, maybe I'm exaggerating a little. Maybe I like to exaggerate a little, but I'd had a tough night.

I fell asleep immediately and dreamed that I was escorting somebody down a street. Then a car pulled up and I realized that the two men in it were about to start shooting at me. I hid behind a parked car, but fell on my side and fired only for water to come out. Damn it if it's not a bloody water pistol I'm holding, I thought, and realized on the instant that I was done for. Only somehow the water pistol changed, in the mysterious way such things can come about in dreams, into a proper gun. I fired twice and got the two thugs who were after me.

Then I woke up.

19

The sun was peeking through the gap in the curtains, and I realized that I was aching like a bastard all over. Then I recalled the events of the night before and figured it was no wonder my body had known happier awakenings.

A glance at my Swatch told me it was coming up to ten in the morning. Time to get up. I didn't much fancy the idea, so I bribed myself with the thought of coffee and a croissant. It was only as I stepped into the living room, en route to the kitchen, that I recalled I'd had a guest staying the night and, wondering if he'd left yet, I looked over to see if he was on the sofa. He was.

And he wasn't about to leave in quite a while.

Not until somebody carried his body out, anyway.

I went over to take a look at him. Just to check my eyes hadn't deceived me.

They hadn't.

He'd been strangled. His eyes were staring up at me with a terrible fixity, and he had turned a decidedly unhealthy shade of pale. I say 'he', but of course it was just a body now. The man who'd once been Javier Fontana had long left it behind.

I laid the back of my hand against the forehead. It was still warm, so the murder couldn't have taken place very long ago. Fortunately there was no blood anywhere, as you would expect, given the nature of the murder.

Whoever had done it couldn't have made much noise coming in, I thought, and he must have attacked Fontana when he was asleep, because I didn't hear a thing.

I went over to the door, to check the lock. It was still bolted. So how did the killer get in? I wondered. Then I saw that the barred iron door that gave onto the balcony was open. Had I not locked it the night before? I couldn't remember doing so. But then, I couldn't remember having opened it, either. And I normally always locked it before going out.

Maybe Fontana opened it in the night, I thought. But why would he do that? I went out onto the balcony and took a look around. A mug had been left on the tiled floor by the side of the lounger. I looked and saw that there was still some tea in it, cold now, of course. On the small table, a packet of Chesterfields had been left along with a silver lighter. The lighter wasn't mine and I don't smoke Chesterfields. Fontana must have woken up and felt restless, so he'd gone out onto the balcony for a cup of tea and a smoke. Then I supposed he'd gone back inside, to take another crack at getting off to sleep and left the door open. And whoever killed him must have climbed up from the garden onto the balcony. It wasn't that far up. The willow tree that conveniently covered my bedroom window, so that I could go around naked with the curtains open if I wanted to of a morning without the neighbours seeing me, would have helped the killer. He could have climbed the tree and then jumped from the branch that was nearest to my balcony. I'd been meaning to tell the man who tended the garden to cut the tree down a little, too, because I suspected it of being a haven for mosquitoes.

I wondered what to do next, and considered calling up Sal Cobos and telling him what had happened. The idea bounced around the walls of my cranium for all of a second or two, before I rejected it. I might know Sal Cobos and chew the cud with him from time to time, but I didn't want to overvalue the stock I had with the man. Not that he's a bad sort or anything. In fact, Sal's a pretty decent all round individual as cops go, but that doesn't mean he isn't still a cop, and I'm sometimes liable to forget that. And sometimes I'd do well *not* to forget that. And I reckoned this was one of those times.

I turned the matter over in my head some more for another minute or so. As I was doing this, it occurred to me that the cops might be on their way here any time now. Because it was a sure bet whoever killed Fontana called the murder in. It seemed to be the way things were working round here just lately.

I had to get rid of the body. But how? It was easier said than done, after all. Was I going to leave the building in broad daylight carrying Fontana's body in a fireman's lift? Somebody would be sure to see me.

Thoughts were buzzing about like a nest of mosquitoes in my head, and I was trying to make sense of them. No, I couldn't just go down in the lift with the body over my shoulder. So what should I do? I realized that I'd better come up with some ideas fast, before the cops showed. But my mind was a blank. Come on, man, I chided myself;

you're supposed to be expert at this sort of thing: making dead bodies disappear and then catching the killer, without the cops being any the wiser. I cursed myself and then I cursed Inge Schwartz. Then it came to me right out of the blue, what I had to do.

I left the flat and used the spare key Mrs. Hopkins had given me to let myself in next door. Mrs. Hopkins is a very nice old English lady who lives alone, has done ever since her husband Michael passed away some six years ago. I had been in the habit of calling in on her from time to time, just to check she was all right and to ask if there was anything she wanted or if there were any odd jobs that might need doing. That explains why she'd given me a spare key. Whenever I went to the supermarket I'd usually buy some groceries for her and I'd use the key to let myself in, if she was out or sleeping when I called, and leave the things I bought in her kitchen. Today was different, though. I hadn't done any shopping for her, and I was hoping she was either sleeping late or out.

I opened the door to her bedroom and heard her snoring away. Then I found the wheelchair that her son used to take her out, when he came over from England. If I were quick then she wouldn't even notice it was gone, I thought, and I left with the wheelchair and returned to my own flat. I found a couple of baseball caps and two pairs of shades, then lifted the body and dropped it into the wheelchair. I slipped the hat and shades onto the dead man, then I put my own on, before I positioned the body so that he was sitting up.

Next I went through the dead man's pockets and found his driving license. I figured his car must be parked nearby. It was just a case of finding it. I considered leaving the body here, and going out in search of Fontana's vehicle. It was a navy-blue Seat Ibiza that he drove. Hardly an uncommon car in this part of the world. But I had the reg, so it shouldn't take me too long to find. Fontana must have parked nearby, after all. Yes, I'll do that, I decided, and had just opened the front door when I heard a police siren.

Realizing there was no time to waste, I dashed back inside and wheeled the body out, then hurried to the lift. I pushed the button and had to wait for the lift to come down. The sirens were getting louder. My heart was pumping hard and loud in my ears. The lift was here. I opened the door and wheeled the body in. It was quite a squeeze, but I managed to get in with him. Then I took it down to the ground floor. A little bell chimed as the lift came to rest. I pushed the door open then wheeled the body out. The police sirens came to a sudden halt, and I realized the squad cars were outside the building. I headed out through the back exit.

A uniform came dashing over, having just emerged from a squad car. 'Morning, sir,' the man said breathlessly. 'Do you live in this block?'

'I do indeed.'

'Did you hear anything unusual earlier or in the night?'

'No, I can't say I did,' I said. 'Why, has something happened?'

'It's all right, sir. Nothing to worry about.'

The man went on into the building through the back entrance, leaving me to go on my way. I was sure he wouldn't recognize me later on. He'd have looked at me and seen a guy in shades and a baseball cap pushing another guy in a wheelchair. That's all he'd be able to tell his superiors, assuming he thought it worth mentioning that he'd spoken to a man as he was leaving the building. I felt confident that I was in the clear as I set off for my car, which I'd left parked up one of the side streets that lead from the *rotunda* or small circular island that the block was built upon, having abandoned my original plan which was to take the dead man's vehicle

Having found my Porsche, I opened the doors then took a quick look around to make sure the coast was clear. It was, so I lifted the body into the back and sat it up. The head fell backwards and, realizing that it looked odd that way and might attract the attention of other motorists, I pulled the body down so that it was slumped in the chair. That's better, I thought. Looks like he's asleep.

I folded the wheelchair and put it in the boot. I looked up the street. There were no coppers in sight. Makes sense, I thought. They're all busy looking for a body back at my place.

When they don't find it, they'll probably think it a little odd, I thought. Then they *will* find it, only later and somewhere else… which they'll no doubt think is even odder.

20

I headed up into the mountains, pulled over by the roadside somewhere beyond Mirjarvo and dumped the body down a ravine. Then I headed back to Bardino. I travelled by the more rustic or scenic route. The roads were narrow and there was a fantastic view from this height down over the coast and out to sea. Not that I was in any mood to be enjoying sea views right then.

Back in the *pueblo*, I parked in the exact same spot I'd left my car in earlier, then headed down to the Café Sevilla on Calle Zaragoza. I had the Colombian waitress, Marta, serve me with orange juice, with coffee in a glass and a toasted roll with tomato and garlic mix in a dish. I scooped the tomato onto the toasted roll with a spoon, then spread it with a knife and poured olive oil on it, in the local style. I read *El Bardinado* while I ate my breakfast. There was nothing about Fontana, my dead journalist friend. Well there wouldn't be yet. It was still too early. I'd have to wait until the evening edition, or else for tomorrow's papers for that. There was an account of the fight I'd had with the charming Vince the night before. The journalist could not be sure as to the cause of the fight. Vince had been sitting with a lady friend, talking peacefully, until yours truly had shown, it said. Then I must have said something or other that Vince took exception too, and the fight broke out. Friends of Vince had got involved, and I was last seen being bundled into a blue BMW. The reg was not known. The said car had set off at speed, so that onlookers had needed to jump out of the road sharpish to avoid being hit. Nobody had any idea where the car was headed. I had not been seen since.

Who was littering my path with corpses and why? I asked myself.

I had no idea. All I knew for sure was that people had suddenly formed a habit of falling dead wherever I was, or wherever I was about to go. I'd been walking on razor blades ever since Inge Schwartz came waltzing into my office that day trailing a breeze of perfume and a storm of sex appeal with her that Strauss would have sold his right hand and the rights to *The Blue Danube* to get to grips with. But she couldn't be trying to set me up, could she? What would she get out of that? What would be the point of it?

It didn't seem to make any sense. My mobile started to buzz and purr. I reached into my jacket pocket and took it out. 'Hello?'

'It's me.' She sounded anxious. 'I need to see you.'

'What's happened?'

'I can't talk over the phone.' Call me Mystic Meg if you like, but somehow I'd just known she was going to say that.

'In that case, I'll see you in my office in ten minutes.'

'No, I think someone may be following me.'

'Where, then?'

'In the lobby of the hotel Las Palmeras.'

'Okay, I'm on my way.'
We hung up.

21

It was only a short distance, so I decided to go there on foot. I walked up to the corner, took a right down to the main road and crossed over. As I did so, I began to get the feeling I was being followed. I headed up the main road, then stopped for a moment and looked in a shop window. I was looking to see the reflection of the mutt that was following me. There. He stopped a little way behind me and looked in a window. Nice one. I entered the shop, which turned out to be one of these all-purpose Chinese stores. I took a tour of the place and checked out the quantity of pots and pans and notepads and diaries and all the other cheap junk in the shop, then came back out and there was the guy who was following me waiting just along the pavement. He was trying hard to look casual. So hard that casual was the last thing he looked. Just to devil the guy, I set off back the way I'd come and then turned the corner to see if he was coming after me. He was. I entered a newsagent's and bought a copy of *El Bardinado*, just for something to do. Then I headed on down to the seafront. As I walked, I took out my mobile and called Inge. 'I'm being followed,' I told her.

'Who by?'

'Dunno yet, but I'm curious to find out,' I said. 'Guy looks like a cop to me.'

'Be careful.'

'You almost sound concerned about me.'

'You are working for me, after all.'

'It's kind of reassuring to know your interest is purely economic. Keeps things simpler that way.' If anything could ever be simple where the likes of this woman was concerned.

'Stop fooling around with me,' she told me off, and I have to confess that a part of me loved it. 'I've got something important to discuss with you.'

'Yes, well I'm on my way, but I may be a little late,' I said. 'That's why I'm calling.'

'You need to shake him off, you mean?'

'Exactly.'

'Make sure you do,' she said.

Then hung up.

I went up to the curb then glanced over my shoulder as I crossed the road, to see if I was still being shadowed. I was. So I cut into the arcade there, at the side of the shoe shop, then ran to my right, past people sitting on the terrace of a café, then took a left and hid round the corner. Peering round the wall, I saw the man come past the café. He was looking from side to side, clearly worried that he'd lost me. I hurried along the narrow road that crossed the arcade, and concealed myself behind the next corner.

Trouble was, I could no longer see if the man was coming after me. Then I noticed that the clothes shop nearby had doors either side of the corner. I entered the shop, sure in the knowledge my shadow couldn't have seen me, then made a show of looking at some T-shirts. I had my chin down, in case the guy happened to glance in through the window, but I was able to keep an eye out for him at the same time.

Perhaps he went the other way, I thought.

But no, there he was.

I let him go past the window, then left the shop through the other door, so I was now behind him. He was short black hair, about five-ten, but stocky, dressed in jeans, white Adidas trainers and a blue sleeveless shirt. That's what I could tell just from looking at the guy. But I was a lot more interested in what I *couldn't* tell that way. Who had sent him, for instance?

There was another cafe up on the next corner, and I figured the tables outside it might come in handy for what I had in mind. I drew level with the man just as we reached the café and shoved him sideways, and he fell over a chair and brought a table down on top of him. As he tried to get up, his face full of fury, I stamped on his hand. He cried out and tried to push himself up on the other side. This time I kicked his wrist. He cried out again.

By now the waiter had come out wanting to know what was going on. When he saw that I was stopping the guy who'd been shadowing me from getting up, he threatened to call the police. 'Go ahead,' I said. Then the owner of the place came out. I know the man. Not well, but I stop by for a drink in his café from time to time, and whenever I do we'll chew the cud about this and that. He's a Londoner, married to a Spanish woman, Rita. Likes to talk to me about the old days, when he used to run a bar in

Soho. He looked at me. 'Arthur,' he said. 'The fuck's going on here?'

'What I'd like to know, Steve,' I said. 'This guy seems to think he's my shadow...been following me everywhere I go.'

'Has he now?' Steve, a balding man in his late thirties, beer belly, tats, looked at me like he understood the situation I was in and was on my side. 'Want me to call the cops?'

'I am a fucking cop, you idiots,' said the shadow.

Steve looked at the man, then he looked at me. I looked at the shadow. 'Some ID might come in handy,' I said.

'I could show it to you, if you'll only stop kicking me.'

'Easy does it,' I told him, and took out my gun.

'You got a license to carry that thing?'

'You bet.'

'You'd better put it away,' he said. 'I've already told you I'm a cop.'

'And I heard you, but I haven't seen any evidence yet.'

He reached into his trousers and brought out a leather pouch, opened it and held it up. I wrested it from the man's hand and took a good look. 'Very nice,' I said.

'So can you stop the fun and games and let me get up now?'

'Sure.' I put my gun away, and helped the man to his feet. But no sooner was he up than he punched me in the gut. The blow took me by surprise. Not only that, but it hurt. I doubled up and must have grunted with the pain.

As I did so, I felt something hit me again and I went flying backwards over a table.

It must have been a pretty good punch, because when I came round I was being helped into the back of a squad car. 'You saw it all, Steve,' I shouted over my shoulder.

'Too fucking right I did, Arthur.'

'I'll need you to come to the station,' I shouted. 'That way they'll have to let me out.'

That was all I had time to say, because the bastard who'd knocked me out pushed me into the back of the car. 'What the fuck is this?' I wanted to know.

'You'll find out,' the beefy bastard said.

'You can't arrest me. I haven't done anything wrong.'

'You assaulted me, for a start. Then you threatened me with a loaded gun. You could be looking at going away for a nice little stretch, amigo.'

'You were following me,' I protested.

'Just doing my job.'

'But there was no way I could've known you were a cop…And I helped you to your feet, once you showed me your ID.'

'That's your story,' Plod replied. 'And anyway, I'm a police officer and you…' He flashed me a nasty wink. 'Well you're not.'

'What were you following me for, anyway?'

'You're a suspect in a murder case,' he said. 'Hadn't you heard? In three murder cases, in fact. Rumour has it dead bodies have a thing for you, seem to like to follow you about. Not so much love as *death* at first sight.'

'I'm a private investigator,' I replied. 'Somebody obviously doesn't like the heat I'm putting on them and wants to cause trouble for me. Hadn't that occurred to you, *agente*?'

'Seems like this person who wants to cause trouble for you's succeeding, *amigo*.'

Very funny, I thought.

'Look,' I tried once more, 'I'm on the same side as you are...'

'I'm a policeman and you're a wannabe... take my advice and study for your *oposiciones,* you want to be a proper cop.'

Seeing that I was getting nowhere, I figured the best thing to do was shut up. So I did.

The cuffs were tight and hurt like a bastard, but I wasn't about to complain. I didn't want to give the two men the satisfaction of telling me it was my own stupid fault for getting myself arrested. Because I knew that's what they'd say. It's probably their favourite line.

22

The cell they put me in had blood and shit on the walls. The décor was nothing particularly new or *avante garde* where I was concerned: I'd seen it before more times than I cared to recall. Even so it was less than pleasant. The pillow was filthy, and there was nothing to read or look at. Nothing to do but pace the small cell, or lie back on the bed and think. I couldn't even look into the corridor, as the two sets of thick bars were designed so as to make it impossible to see through them to either side.

I'd been in a cell like this before, of course, and so it wasn't really such a big deal. But it was irritating all the same, and I felt frustrated and impotent, powerless. Which I suppose is how I was meant to be feeling, because that's the whole point of putting somebody in a cell.

I was in there for the best part of the day, and then my lawyer, Carmen Gordano, finally showed. Carmen is tall, slim and kind of elegant in a quietly terrifying sort of way; but far more important so far as I'm concerned, she's sharp as a whip. Once I'd explained to her what had happened, she arranged for us to go up and have an interview with Sal Cobos. Sal had mellowed a little since the last time I'd spoken to him but not so much that he wasn't prepared to stick up for his colleague. 'I dunno what you expect, Arthur,' he said. 'You punched a police officer and then proceeded to kick him and stamp on his hands, so as to make it impossible for him to get up... Then you brought out a gun and threatened him with it.'

'He was following me,' I said. 'And I have witnesses who can vouch for the fact that I helped him up once he'd shown me his ID. Then he punched me twice, and knocked me out with the second one.'

'You're getting soft, Arthur.' Sal grinned. 'Whatever's happening to you? I remember the days when you used to be able to take a punch.'

'I object to the way you're addressing my client, Inspector Jefe,' Carmen said. 'He isn't some punch bag that your officers can use for boxing practice. He's a victim of assault by a police officer, and you're treating it as a joke which makes it worse.' She played her part so well that you could almost feel the gravity of the situation weighing you down. 'Quite frankly, I'm shocked to find that this is what you and your force have come to,' she went on. 'I'd like to know what the Minister in charge of this sort of thing would make of it.'

Cobos's eyes nearly left their sockets at the mention of the Minister. Good old Carmen, I could have placed a hand either side of her head and planted a smacker of a kiss on her lips at that point. I do like a strong woman. Particularly when she's my lawyer and I'm in a mess that she's trying to get me out of.

'I'm sorry,' Cobos said. 'It's just that Arthur and I go way back.'

'That doesn't give you the right to treat him with the sort of familiarity you'd ascribe to a doormat.' Carmen's outrage was on the point of going viral. 'That's the kind of logic men use to justify themselves when they launch physical attacks upon their wives.' While I'm not totally sure that I enjoyed playing the role of the abused 'wife' in this cozy little scenario that Carmen was working up, I had to give her full marks for theatricality and verbal wizardry. She was a true master of her trade: a bullshitter *par excellence.*

23

I listened starry-eyed as my heroine of the hour, my cavalry and my Zorro said, 'My client has witnesses who can vouch for the fact that he was attacked, and I really must insist that he be released immediately.'

Sal Cobos held up his hand. 'Okay, okay,' he said. 'Maybe the officer played a little unfair, but nobody likes to get punched and kicked.' Cobos sat back in his padded swivel chair, frowned, tented his fingers. I sensed that he was all out of ideas and merely trying to recover from the whirlwind of words he'd just been subjected to, courtesy of Carmen, and that he was merely pretending to ponder the situation. I could almost have felt sorry for the man, if I'd been so inclined. But I didn't and wasn't.

'So I take it I'm free to go, Sal, right?' I said.

'For now,' he said.

I got up and made to leave, along with Carmen.

'Oh and Arthur,' he called to me, as I got to the door. 'Try not to let any more dead bodies show up around you, will you? It's getting more than a little difficult for me to call the dogs off.'

I tried to think of *something* to say in response; something that would give me the last word and cut Sal dead, but nothing sprang to mind. I was tired and my mind was a blank. So I just turned and went on my way.

I retrieved my things—my mobile, keys, wallet—and signed for them; then, on the way out, Carmen asked me if I wanted to press charges. 'What for?' I asked her.

'Assault, unlawful arrest, abuse of police power, and whatever else we can cook up...'

I laughed.

'What's so funny?' she asked me.

'I'm a private investigator.'

'So?'

'A dick can't take the cops to court.'

'If he's got witnesses he can.'

'They'd soon find a way to put me out of business.'

'But if you've really got a solid witness, as you say you have, you'd win.'

'You don't understand,' I said. 'Cops are sore losers. It gets to go with the cop mentality. Besides there are lots of them, and there's only one of me. If I won my battle in court, I'd soon find myself in a never-ending war with only one loser—yours truly... No, it would only screw things up for me all the more.'

'You're your own worst enemy, do you know that?'

'I should do by now.'

'What does that mean?' Carmen asked.

'I lost count years ago of how many people have told me that same thing.'

'The people who told you it were right, Arthur,' she replied. 'They were trying to get you to look out for your own interests.'

'Look, Carmen,' I said, 'you're a great lawyer but–'

'You don't want me to do my job.'

'You've already done it... you got me out of the cell, and that's all I wanted.'

I kissed her on either cheek and thanked her again, and then I went out.

24

There was a warm balmy breeze blowing up, and it felt good to be out in the open air and free to enjoy the rest of the evening after having spent the best part of the day banged up.

I walked along for a bit, then crossed over and zigzagged my way down to Tahiti, a bar I sometimes use on the seafront. I found myself a vacant table, sat at it, and listened to the boom of the Mediterranean and smelt the salt sea air. I studied the drinks menu and considered trying a Mind-blowing Orgasm, but the conservative in me won the day and I went for a Manhattan instead. It went down well – so well, I had the pretty Spanish waitress bring me another, and I had just sipped it when my mobile began to ring. I took it out. Surprise, surprise, I thought, when I saw who was calling. 'What's up this time?'

'I need to speak to you,' she said.

'Well I don't recall trying to stop you.'

'There's no need to take that tone with me.'

'What tone would that be?'

'There you go again,' she said. 'It's like you want to poke fun at me.'

'Well the feeling's mutual, I'm sure.'

'And what exactly does that mean?'

'You have been leading me on something of a wild goose chase of late, I seem to recall.'

'Look,' she said, 'I'm paying you to work for me...or I thought I was.'

'Oh you've paid me all right. But not enough for what I've had to go through to earn it. I've been required to allow myself to be framed for three murders, and I've been dangled head first into a swimming pool inhabited by a hungry great white shark. I've been shot at and accused of murder by the local police and thrown in a cell... Now the way I see it, Inge, I think we could say you've been getting your money's worth, don't you?'

She hung up. As I figured she would. Her type always does. But then she called me back again a minute later. As her type also always does.

'The matter, I said, your temper get the better of you?'

'I just don't know how you can seem so nice at times and then be so abominably rude, like you were just then.'

'If some of the things I've been through happened to you, Inge, then I'm sure you'd be a little rude, too.'

'Okay,' she said, 'maybe you've a right to be a little angry... But everything has its limits.'

'You're too right it does Inge, and right now one of the things that's reached its particular limit is my patience.' I hung up, just for the sheer pleasure of being the one to do it.

She called me back immediately.

'What?'

'How dare you hang up on me?'

'You hung up on me first,' I said.

'Do you always act like this with women?'

'Act like what?'

'Do whatever the woman does?'

'No, only sometimes. Why–where's the problem in that, anyway? Men and women are equal nowadays, haven't you heard?'

'We're equal, but that doesn't make us the same,' she said. 'If I put my lipstick on, does it mean you're going to put some on, too?'

I laughed and said, 'As we were saying a moment ago, Inge, everything has its limits.'

'I need to talk to you.'

'So go ahead and talk.'

'Not over the phone,' she said.

'And what's this about a Rembrandt?'

'What?'

'One Vicente Caportorio seems to be under the impression you own one, and he wants it.'

'Where are you?'

'Do you?'

'Yes, but I'll explain about that when we meet up. Where are you?'

I told her.

'Don't go anywhere. I'll be there as soon as I can.'

So I stayed put and waited. I finished my Manhattan and ordered another while I did so. I was halfway through it when she showed.

She was wearing a peach-coloured dress that showed off her figure to perfection. The slender waist and full bust. Boy oh boy. But that wasn't all. She walked with the easy rhythm of a cat and she had about her the slightly haughty air that is common to beautiful women. It's hard to say what it is exactly. Something about the way she held her head so erect, on the long slender stalk she had for a her neck. *You can look but don't think you can touch* was the general gist of the message she gave out. 'Take a seat,' I said.

She looked as though she were unsure as to whether she ought to, but then she parked herself on the plastic chair. She fixed me with a serious look, her eyes two blue gems, cold but beautiful. 'You're sure we're not being watched?'

'Not to the best of my knowledge.'

She looked at the glass I'd just held to my lips and said, 'How many of those have you had?'

'Is that any of your business?'

'I can't see why I shouldn't be able to take an interest in whether or not you're sober, seeing as I'm paying your fee.'

'I'm sober enough.'

'You would say that.'

'I'm the one who's doing the work, right?'

She battened her eyelids and gave me a schoolteacherish look. 'If you say so,' she said.

'I say so.'

'Okay,' she said, 'there's no need to raise your voice.'

'What's all this about a Rembrandt?' I asked her in a quieter voice.

'It's true,' she said. 'I inherited one.'

'What do you know about this guy Vince Caportorio?'

'Who?'

'He's a gangster.'

'I can assure you that I've never mixed with types like that.'

'Well he knows who you are, and what's more he knows you own a Rembrandt and he sounds as though he's very interested in finding out where you're keeping it.'

'I'm in rather a frightening situation right now.' She brushed a few stray strands of hair out of her eyes. 'I feel as though you're the only person I can depend on, Arthur.' She gave me the old up-from-under look. She'd probably practiced it on a thousand and one other guys before she'd got to me, but somehow that didn't matter. 'I can depend on you, can't I?'

'Of course.'

'You can be rather sweet at times,' she said. 'When you want to be.'

Something turned over in my chest again, and I knew I had to fight against it.

She took a quick glance around, as if she half expected that she were being watched. Which she was, of course, but only in the way that a girl who looks the way she looked can never go anywhere without being watched.

'How about you finish your drink and pay,' she said, 'and we take a little hike along the seafront.'

'Sure.'

I knocked back what was left in my glass and signaled to the waitress and paid my bill. Then we got up and set off.

25

We crossed over, and walked along by the wall that separates pavement from beach. She walked quickly, with her chin up and I could hear the heels of her court shoes beating out a fierce tattoo as we moved along. She was frowning, too, I noticed, like something was eating at her.

'Has something happened?' I asked.

'You could say that.'

'Well are you going to tell me?'

'Let's go somewhere a little quieter.'

We walked right to the end and crossed the modern bridge they've built there that goes over the canal. There were children down below in the water riding with their parents in little paddleboats shaped like swans and ducks. To the side of the canal there was an outdoor café, and further up there was a small play area with a roundabout and swings. We crossed the bridge and went past the old castle, which had recently been restored so as to serve as a tourist attraction, and it wasn't until we'd passed the new hotel, with its domes and minarets all done in the Arabic style, that she led me down onto the beach. It was almost deserted at this hour, although I could see a young couple sitting down by the water's edge.

'I think we're alone now,' I said, 'so if you've got something to tell me I think you'd better hurry up and get it off your chest.'

'I don't know what to do, Arthur.' Her voice sounded brittle, like it was about to break into a shriek.

'Do about what?'

'They've got her.'

'Who has?'

'If I knew the answer to that I'd tell you.'

'You mean you've got evidence that Gisela's been abducted?'

She nodded and then the next moment she threw herself on me, and I held her close and smelt her jasminey scent. Maybe she was full of lies and was taking me for a fool, but even so I felt at that moment like I was prepared to go to the ends of the earth for her. I would be her St. George and do battle with the dragon, if that's what she wanted. 'Do you always offer your clients this kind of service, Arthur?' she sighed.

'Not usually,' I whispered in her ear.

'So what's different about me, then?'

'You're not my usual kind of client.'

'How come?'

'You're more gorgeous than the rest of them.'

'Is that all it is?'

I didn't know and I didn't care. I gazed deep into her eyes, that were black in the reflection of the moon, and then I kissed her on the mouth. She didn't seem to be bored or show any signs of wanting me to stop, so I just carried on. When we finally came up for air, I realized that it wasn't just the sound of the sea and the stars and the balmy breeze and her jasmine scent that had got to me—although I'm sure all of those things provided a helping hand—but there was more to it, a lot more. I was hooked on her, whether I liked it or not. And if I were honest with myself, then I'd have to admit that right now I liked it. I liked it a lot. Why, I'd even stopped calling myself a fool, which was a really bad sign, I know. But there you are. I'm not the first guy to fall for a gorgeous girl, and I sure as hell won't be the last. If I was an idiot, then I was no more of one than a long list of other guys. Of course I had this thing about wanting to appear tough. It was part of the image of the job, I suppose. And a part of me couldn't see how my slavering over Little Miss Butter Wouldn't Melt like a puppy that has just got its mitts on its first bone fitted in with the tough guy role I was playing. Although it wasn't as simple as that, either; because I'm no weed. I mean, I don't like to boast, but I really *am* a pretty tough sort of guy. It's just that I've got my weak spots, I guess. And Little Miss Butter Wouldn't Melt here had found them all.

I made an effort to pull myself together. 'You were telling me about Gisela,' I said.

'Yes,' she sighed.

'But you don't know who's taken her?'

'No.'

'Somebody's been in contact with you, though?'

She nodded and buried her face in my lapel. I felt her body judder and heard her sobs. 'She's been kidnapped.'

26

I wondered if Vince Caportorio might be behind this recent development. Right now, he was my star suspect on a list of one.

'It's okay,' I said. 'I'll get her back for you.'

She lifted her head and looked at me. 'Will you really, Arthur?'

'Yes.'

'Promise me.'

'Cross my heart and hope to die,' I said.

'Oh Arthur,' she sighed. 'I'm so lucky to have found you.'

I wasn't sure what to say to that. In fact, I wasn't at all sure that I could make good on my promise. How could I be, after all? But she needed reassurance, and nothing good ever comes from acting as though you lack confidence.

She gave me her up-from-under look again. 'I can trust you, Arthur, can't I?' she said. 'I'm mean, you're not just spinning me a line, to make me feel better, right?'

'No, of course not.' I was going to get her sister Gisela back if it was the last thing I did, even though I had no idea how I was going to do it. 'I need you to tell me everything you know.'

She dried her eyes with the backs of her hands. 'I'm sorry if I've appeared to be a little...emotional.'

What was I meant to say in response to that? Was I supposed to forgive her for bringing me to this lonely part of the beach and throwing herself on my neck, and then letting me kiss her the way I had?

'You must think I'm a perfect fool,' she said, looking away in the direction of the breaking waves.

'Why do you say that?'

'I've behaved like one and we both know it, so there's no need for you to deny it, Arthur.' There was something rather quaint about the way she said my name. Although I suppose Arthur is a pretty old-fashioned sounding moniker. If you shorten it to Art it can sound kind of with-it and funky. But Arthur is old school. It's black-and-white movies and high tea with scones. It sounds rather prim and faintly ridiculous, I've often thought.

She gave me the benefit of her up-from-under look again. 'Well don't rush to my defense, will you?' she said. 'Just because I say you don't have to deny it when I say I've behaved like a perfect fool doesn't mean you have to take me at my word.'

I laughed.

'My sister has been kidnapped and you think it's funny?'

'How about we give the amateur dramatics a rest, Inge, and you tell me what you know?'

She slapped my cheek. It stung a little.

'I hope that made you feel better?' I said.

'It did. But only a little.'

'You're a feisty little thing under that glossy exterior.'

'You make me sound like a magazine.'

I thought she looked like she ought to be *in* a magazine, but I wasn't in a mood to tell her that after being slapped. 'So are you going to tell me what exactly the kidnapper said to you?'

'He wants something from me.'

'They usually do.'

'You needn't sound so cool and callous about it.'

'Sorry, that wasn't my intention,' I said. 'What is it that he wants?'

'A painting.'

I was having to drag the information out of her, sentence by sentence. 'It wouldn't be a Rembrandt by any chance?'

'You got it in one.'

'Do you know who the kidnapper is?'

'No.'

'It's Vince Caportorio,' I said. 'It's got to be.'

'Who's he?'

'He's a local gangster,' I said. 'I asked you earlier if you knew of him. He's the guy who wanted to feed me to a shark and sent his two mutts to kill me and dispose of my body.'

'Whether you're right or wrong about the kidnapper's identity doesn't really help us much.' She shrugged. 'I mean he's got Gisela, and so I have to give him what he wants or he's going to kill her.'

I figured she probably had a point. 'Has he told you where and when he wants the painting delivered?'

'No, only that he's going to call me again tomorrow, and when he does he's going to tell me then. But he did say I'm to have the painting with me, ready to be delivered to him an hour after he calls.'

'And do you have it with you?'

'I have it where I can get it by tomorrow, yes.'

27

I looked at her again. I'd never met anyone quite like her. Not anyone who was as beautiful as her, to begin with. Or anyone who could muster up a Rembrandt, or have one handy, waiting in the wings in case of an emergency. Rembrandts are fairly rare and expensive articles, after all. This all struck me as being ridiculously outlandish, like something out of a book or film. Then again, Inge herself was like something out of a book or film - and not just any book or film, either, but an outlandish one. You only had to take one look at her to see that. 'You didn't tell me that you owned a Rembrandt,' I said.

'You never asked, Arthur... Besides, so what if I do? What's that got to do with anything?'

'Quite a lot, by the sound of things.'

'It does *now*,' she said. 'But it didn't when I first came to you... I mean, I didn't know Gisela had been kidnapped then, did I?'

'What Rembrandt is it, anyway?'

'It's a self-portrait.' When she lifted her chin and looked at me there was a pitiful expression in her eyes. 'You will help me, Arthur, won't you?'

'Of course... But what do you want me to do?' I asked her. 'Do you want me to hand over the Rembrandt to the kidnapper?'

'I don't see that we have much choice, do you?'

'No, I guess not,' I said. 'But how is it that you've got a Rembrandt in your possession?'

'It's been in the family for several generations.'

'If you're from a rich family,' I said, 'then what was your sister doing living in the Bocanazo and working in a bar on the seafront?'

'Who knows?' She wiped her nose and shrugged. 'She was trying to find herself, I suppose.'

'Why'd she come to Bardino of all places to do that, do you think?'

'Why shouldn't she come here?' she replied. 'It doesn't always have to be India that people go to, to discover their inner self, you know. Not everyone's John Lennon.'

'But even so, Bardino is the last place most people would come.'

'Well it doesn't seem so bad to me.'

'Maybe that's because you haven't been here long enough to get a good look at what goes on.'

'Everyone who lives here can't be a rotter, surely, can they?'

'Can't they?' I grinned. 'You could have fooled me.'

'Well you live here, Arthur.'

'Don't I just.'

'And you're not a rotter, are you?'

'I figure that would be a matter of opinion.'

'I certainly don't think you are, anyway,' she said and gave me the old dove-eyed look that was supposed to melt your heart. This girl knew her way around a man's mind the way a grandmaster knows his way around a chessboard. I could almost feel her fiddling with my pieces.

We both fell silent a moment, then Inge ran her hand over my lapel. 'So you will do it?' she asked.

'Make the exchange, you mean?'

She nodded.

I realized that there were only really two answers to this question: yes or no. While our thoughts and feelings can be subject to an infinity of shades of grey, to invoke the old cliché, the world of the private dick has a distinctly Manichean flavour: one elects either to act or not to do so. I was either in on this one or I wasn't. And if I wasn't then I figured I was *out*, so far as Inge Schwartz would be concerned, which is to say I'd be off the case. Now as you have probably gathered by now, I had a whole bucket-load of doubts and questions floating around in my head where Inge was concerned, but I was more than a little gone on her and so the bucket had sort of gone out the window. Besides, I wanted to follow the investigation to its natural conclusion. Right now, I was half way to nowhere and I didn't like the feeling it gave me. The fact that I could use the money was the very least of it. So there was really only one answer I was ever going to give to Inge's question. 'Sure,' I said. 'First you'll have to give me the Rembrandt, though, and tell me where to take it and when.'

'I'll let you know, don't worry. But I'll need you to be ready to drop everything at the drop of a hat.'

'No problem.'

'Thanks. You know you can be very good and nice when you want to be, Arthur.'

I felt like a little kid who's just been praised by the Sunday school teacher he has a secret crush on.

'I'm tired,' she said. 'I'm going to go and get some sleep now. Tomorrow's going to be a busy day.'

'Call me as soon as the kidnapper's contacted you.'

'Okay.'

She set off over the sand, and I watched her move in silhouette from the light of the moon, a cutout figure carrying my heart in her hands. What's that line from the poem where the guy urges his ladylove to tread carefully because it's his dreams she's walking on?

I don't know how long I stood there, but she was well out of sight before I went home and turned in for the night.

28

I was woken up the following morning by the sound of my mobile ringing. I dug it out of my pocket and saw if it was who I thought it was. Then wondered what she wanted as I said, '*Hola*, sweetness.'

'Arthur, you've got to help me,' she said, sounding all breathy with excitement, as if she'd been running. 'I'm being followed.'

'Where are you?'

'I'm sitting outside a café on Calle Soroya… I wondered what the man who's following me would do, if I came and sat at a table.'

'What did he do?'

'He's sitting at a table not far away.'

'Maybe he likes the cut of your jib.'

'My jib…?'

'Well your skirt, then…'

'He doesn't look like a tailor to me.'

'You know what I meant.'

'I know what you meant, Arthur,' she said. 'But I wish you'd stop being so facetious. It's as if you like to poke fun at me all the time.' Maybe I do, I thought. But seeing as I'd been putting my life on the line for the lady ever since I'd agreed to work for her, I felt I had the right at least to engage in a little light banter. 'I'm being serious, Arthur,' she said. 'Now are you going to help me? Or are you just in a mood to carry on making fun of me and laughing at my expense?'

I told her that I was being serious. 'You're not an unattractive little package, after all,' I went on. 'I mean, the idea may not have crossed your mind, what with how sweet and innocent you are and everything, Inge, but there could be men out there who'd take a certain pleasure from looking at you.'

'He's doing more than just looking at me, Arthur. He's *following* me, like I just told you.' She sounded nervous, too: her voice had an edgy brittle quality to it, like a violin whose strings are too taut. 'I'm convinced he's been sent by the kidnapper,' she said. 'Maybe the man's plan is to intercept me once I've gone to pick up the Rembrandt, then they won't even have to hand Gisela over, will they?'

'It's not the way kidnappers normally work.'

'I wouldn't know about that.'

'Just try to stay calm.'

'I'm trying to, Arthur. But I'm frightened.'

'Okay,' I said. 'Stay where you are and I'll come over and meet you.'

'Are you sure that's wise?' she said. 'Once this man sees you he'll know what you look like, won't he?'

'So?'

'How are you going to be able to help me, then?'

'So what do you want me to do exactly?'

'I was thinking it might be wiser if you were to go and pick up the Rembrandt for me, Arthur,' she said. 'Would you do that for me?'

'I guess so, if you'd care to tell me where it is.'

'I can trust you not to run off with it, though, Arthur, can't I?'

I laughed at that one.

'What's so funny?'

'If I were going to disappear with it, then I'd hardly tell you, now would I?'

'No, I don't suppose you would.'

We both went quiet a moment. I figured she must trust me all right and I wondered why. I mean okay, I was a private dick and I was supposed to be working for her, sure; but if I were to disappear with this Rembrandt of hers then the chances were, if I played my cards right and knew how to fence it properly, I'd never have to work again. Inge interrupted my train of thought, saying, 'I suppose it was a silly question, you're right, Arthur. But I'm nervous and frightened. I've never been in a situation like this before, and I don't know who to trust.'

'Well I'm afraid I can't really help you there, sweetness,' I replied. 'I mean you're either going to have to trust yours truly or you're well and truly screwed.'

'It would appear that way.'

'You don't sound too happy about it.'

'Would you be?'

'I really don't know how to reply to that question, Inge–except to say that I didn't get my licence to practice as a private investigator by stealing from my clients.'

'No, I'm sure you didn't, Arthur,' she said. 'But I'm equally sure that it's not every day that you have a client who asks you to pick up an original Rembrandt for her. You could run off and sell it, then you'd never have to work again.'

So she'd finally got round to considering this possibility, I thought. But of course she had. What kind of a fool did she take me for? 'Gee, you're right,' I said. 'You know, I'd never thought of that, but now you're starting to give me ideas...'

'Now you're mocking me again.'

'Sorry, but it's the line I tend to take with people who insult me.'

'But I didn't insult you, did I?'

'No... not unless calling somebody a liar and a thief passes for paying them a compliment nowadays... Although, given where we are, maybe it does.'

'What on earth are you talking about, Arthur?'

'Don't you read the newspapers over here?'

'What?'

'They're practically all at it.'

'All at what?'

'Never mind,' I said. 'So do you want me to help you, or don't you?'

'Yes, I do.'

'You mean you've made up your mind?'

'Yes, I think I have.'

'You think you have, or you have?'

'I have.'

'That was quick,' I said. 'Don't tell me, you remembered looking into my honest baby blues and knew that I was the man for the job, right?'

'Something like that, Arthur.'

'Good, well in that case, perhaps you'd like to stop taking me for a chump, seeing as I'm supposed to be working for you.'

'What do you mean by that?'

'I mean that you can cut the sweet and innocent act, Inge, because it just doesn't wash with me. It didn't wash the first time you tried it on me and it's been working a little less every time since then.'

'I really don't know where you've got your manners from,' she bit back at me; 'but quite frankly I don't think I've ever been spoken to in such a rude fashion in all my life.'

'You can blame the teachers at my old alma mater, Eton.'

'I've heard of that school,' she replied. 'Isn't it supposed to be one of the better ones?'

'So they say,' I said. 'Anyway, are we going to waste time talking about my schooldays or are you going to tell me where I've got to go?'

She went quiet for a moment, as if she needed time to consider whether or not she could trust me; or maybe she'd simply taken a moment out to powder her nose. Then she said, 'Have you got pen and paper handy?'

'Sure. Fire away.'

She gave me a set of directions and instructions that she'd clearly thought out in advance. Then she said, 'And make sure nobody follows you there, okay?'

'Don't worry. I've got a lot of experience at this sort of thing.'

29

I was to go to the Hotel Belmondo on Calle Ronda, and pick up a key that she'd left in reception.

It was just a five-minute walk, and turned out to be a three-star establishment with flags hanging over the entrance. The flags seemed to confer an air of diplomacy on the place that had little to do with the ordinary running of a hotel, so far as I could make out. The man in the reception–skinny, mid-forties and wearing a purplish waistcoat with a white shirt, bowtie and not much hair on top–was reading a newspaper, and he looked up at me with a sort of studied suspicion for a moment. Then he put the newspaper down and asked me if I wanted a room. I shook my head and told him that a Señorita Schwartz had sent me over. She had left a key for me to pick up. The man nodded. Yes, he'd been expecting me. He turned and reached up to take a small manila envelope from one of the cubbyholes that covered the wall. 'Here you are, sir.'

I opened the envelope and, sure enough, there was a key inside. I thanked the man and went out in search of a taxi. It didn't take me too long to find one, and I skipped in the back and told the driver to take me over to the Bocanazo. As the cab pulled away, I looked through the back window, to see if we were being followed. We weren't. Minutes later, we pulled up outside of the building I'd been told to go to. I paid the fare, then got out and took a look around, just to check there was nobody on my tail. There didn't seem to be. Just to make extra sure, I decided to take a turn round the block before I entered the building. It was the next block along from the one I'd come to before that time, in search of Gisela Schwartz, and it was built upon the same design. There was no elevator, so I climbed the stairs.

Many of the residents were Moroccans or else from Eastern Europe: economic migrants who'd come here to try and better their lot but hadn't succeeded in doing so to any great degree so far. At any rate, it was a strange place for the daughter of a rich man to choose to come and live. And an even stranger place to hide a Rembrandt. Or maybe it wasn't so strange, I thought. Maybe Inge had figured that a rundown block in the Bocanazo was the last place anyone would look. Of course her sister Gisela had been living in the next block, but Inge assured me that nobody who knew Gisela knew about this second flat. It was a two-bedroom number, she said, and she'd only started to rent it a few days ago. Whether she lived in the place, or had just rented it for a short period in order to have somewhere to store the Rembrandt, I wasn't sure. We didn't go into details on the phone. She had been nervous and keen for me to go and pick up the painting as soon as possible.

I found the door and slipped the key into the lock. It fit. I turned it and pushed, and the door opened. So far, so good.

I had my gun in my hand as I entered the flat, and I held it up in front of me as I took a look around. I remembered what had happened the last time I'd come to the Bocanazo, and I didn't want to be caught out the same way again. I moved with the slow, deliberate, light-footed caution of a big cat as I went through the flat.

The door opened directly into the living room, and there was nobody in it. There was a sofa upholstered in caramel-coloured imitation leather, and there was a hard chair over by the window. In front of the sofa there was a coffee table, which looked like it was made of deal. There was an empty ashtray on it. The television faced the sofa, and there was one of those consul cabinets behind it. The cabinet was affixed to the wall, and took up most of it. There were a number of little knickknacks on it of the sort you can pick up for a song in the markets or the local Chinese shops.

The place smelt of dust, and seemed like it hadn't been lived in for quite a time. Maybe Inge Schwartz wasn't planning on living here after all, I thought, recalling now that she'd told me she only rented the place out 'a few days ago'. Had she rented it for the sole purpose of hiding the Rembrandt here? In many ways it might be the last place anyone would look for a priceless painting.

The flat was built on the same design as the one my client's sister had rented, in the next block along. There was a kitchen, off to the left. I kicked the door open and crouched with my feet placed well apart, and holding my gun out with both hands, ready to fire if I needed to. I didn't. There was nobody in the kitchen. It was a rather basic and gloomy oblong-shaped affair, with sky-blue painted walls. The fridge was humming away noisily.

I turned slowly to my right, and moved up the small hallway that ran off the living room. There were four doors on it, two of them closed and the other two were ajar. I kicked the one immediately to my right all the way open, and looked in at what was the bathroom. There was nobody in it. I did the same with the other doors, and checked there was nobody standing behind them, waiting to hit me with something or point a gun at me. There wasn't. I checked in the wardrobes, just to make sure, and under the bed. I wouldn't say I was paranoid, but after what happened the last time I came to this part of town I certainly reckoned it was wise to err on the side of caution.

Having satisfied myself that I was alone in the place, I went back over to the television, in the living room. On top of it there were two control units, one for the DVD player and the other for the television. I turned both television and DVD on, then I looked under the sofa and found the DVD that Inge had told me would be there. I took it out of its case and fed it into the DVD player, then pushed *Play*. The screen was full of snow for a few moments, and then Inge's face appeared. 'If you're watching this, then it's because you'll have been sent here by me. In which case, you'll be wanting to know where it is. Listen carefully.'

30

I did more than listen. I wrote down the directions that she gave. Then I took the DVD out, slipped it back into its case and returned it to its place under the sofa. I turned the television and DVD off, too, figuring I might as well leave everything as I'd found it. Then I left the Bocanazo and walked back over to the block where I lived. It was only a few minutes' on foot, even though it was light years away in terms of the economic and social status of its residents and the quality of the houses and flats they lived in. I found my Porsche, climbed in and set off on the road out of Bardino. It wasn't long before I was heading up into the mountains for the village of Magro. I'd heard of the place, but had never been there. It was a forty-five minute drive along narrow, twisting mountain roads, and it wasn't the sort of place you'd want to come back from late at night after a few drinks. Make a slip and you could easily find yourself shooting off over the edge of a cliff. Goodnight, Irene. Go take the long sleep nobody wakes up from, why don'tcha?

If you had the guts to look out of the side window and the time to appreciate such things, then I'm sure the landscape was spectacular in its own dry and rugged kind of way. High up over the mountains in the distance, I could see what from the size of its wingspan must be an eagle wheel-arching its way over the landscape.

I drove with the windows down, and the sun seemed to get hotter and meaner the further inland I went. Then I got a glimpse of the village, just beyond the hill in front of me. It turned out to be a tiny affair: just a matter of a few streets converging on a main square with a church and a couple of bars and restaurants. I pulled over, then got out of the Porsche and stretched. So this is Magro, I thought. The sun bounced off the white walls of the houses and other buildings, and I found myself screwing my eyes up in a squint behind my Ray Bans. At a first glance, the village looked like an unusual location for a woman like Inge Schwartz to spend her time.

I was after number 11. It was on the main street, she said. I found the house and put the key in the door. It fit. I turned it. The door opened. So far, so good. I entered the house warily. The place smelt of dust, and you could tell it hadn't been lived in for quite a while. The curtains were drawn and so it was dark, or at least relatively so, and the contrast after the brightness of the sunlit street outside blinded me temporarily. So I stood there by the door, with my gun up, ready for anything. Anything didn't happen. In fact nothing did, which may or may not be the same thing. As my eyes gradually adjusted to the light, or comparative lack of it, I saw that I was standing in a large living room. There was a tiled floor, with a leather three-piece suite and a television and video over in the corner. The walls had all been painted white, and by and large they seemed to have stayed that way. There was a large stone fireplace and, in the recesses either side of it, floor to ceiling pinewood shelves had been fitted. The shelves were empty but for a few paperbacks.

The door in the wall off to the left was ajar. I gave it a nudge with my toe. It moved. I found myself looking in at the kitchen. Tiled floor, pinewood worktops, new-looking cooker, fridge, washing machine. Nobody in there. I opened the door to the next room, which had a large double bed in it. The bed had a metal frame with a big imitation-porcelain bauble at each corner. It had been made up and was covered with a quilt done in a floral pattern. It didn't look like it had been slept in for quite a while.

I went in and checked out the *en suite* bathroom. It was fairly big and was equipped with a shower, toilet, sink and bathtub. Nobody in there, either. I went over to the fireplace, which looked as though it had never been used, got down on my haunches and reached an arm in, as I'd been directed. Sure enough, there was a little lever in there, right at the back. It was hidden out of sight, so that you'd never find it unless you were told it was there. I yanked it, and the shelves to my left moved away from the wall. There was a little recess area with a safe in it, just as Inge had said there would be.

I played with the nob on the front, twisting it this way and that, so as to feed in the combination she'd given me, and sure enough it opened.

31

I reached in and took it out, taking care to pick it up by the frame. It was covered with sackcloth, which I carefully removed, and then I found myself looking at a portrait of Rembrandt as an old man. He looked tired in the painting, beleaguered, weighed down by the quantity of junk the world had thrown at him. It was all there in the eyes. They were full of a knowing sadness, almost as though they pitied you, the viewer. They were eyes that had seen a lot of the world - too much of it, perhaps.

I heard voices outside the window. I took my gun back out of its holster, and I stood there pointing it at the door, waiting. But then the voices became less distinct, as their owners must, I presumed, have passed on up the street. I reminded myself that I was standing in a house that was situated on the main street in the village, a fact that I'd forgotten for a moment, so caught up was I with the painting I was holding in my hand and my own thoughts. It was only to be expected that people would pass up and down past the window there, but the curtains were drawn and so nobody could see in.

I told myself not to be so jumpy and put the Rembrandt back in the sackcloth, then went and peeped through the curtains out at the street. It all looked quiet enough out there, so I left the house and made my way the short distance back to my Porsche. I opened the boot and put the

Rembrandt in there, then I climbed in behind the wheel and set off back the way I'd come. I hadn't gone far before my mobile began to ring. I took my right hand off the wheel and reached into my jacket. '*Hola?*'

'Where are you?'

It was Inge and she sounded anxious, uptight.

'I've just picked it up,' I said. 'Now I'm driving back to you. I left the village just a few minutes ago.'

'Good.'

'Are you still being tailed?'

'Yes.'

'Same guy?'

'He's on the corner opposite.'

'Where are you now?'

'At the hotel,' she said. 'He followed me back here. It makes me nervous, the thought of him out there.'

'And it's always the same guy that's been following you, is it?'

'Yes,' she replied. 'You don't think he could be the kidnapper?'

'No, that would be too easy. I mean, the man who's got Gisela would have to be stupid to work that way... he must have this guy working for him.' I suspected the kidnapper was Vince Caportorio and the man on Inge's tail was one of the gangster's mutts. 'Has he called you again?'

'I was going to tell you,' she said. 'He called a few minutes ago.'

'And?'

'He wants to make the exchange this evening at nine o'clock.'

'Where?'

'He's going to call me again at eight and tell me,' she said. 'I told him about you and said you'd be coming with me. He agreed to that, but said if he gets the slightest whiff of a cop the deal's off and we'll never see Gisela again.'

'Did you tell him who I am?'

'No, I just said that you're a friend of the family.'

'Good,' I said. 'Well I don't have a problem with forgetting to call in the cops if you don't.'

'I'd never be able to look myself in the mirror again if we did and the kidnapper found out and killed my sister.'

'How did you get him to agree to allow you to take me along?'

'I told him I can't drive and that I'd be too frightened to go through with a thing like that on my own in any case.'

'What did he have to say to that?'

'He said he'd kill Gisela if I didn't go along with what he said, and I said I was sure he'd kill us both if I were to go there on my own.'

'Nice negotiating style you have, Inge.'

'I wasn't aware I was negotiating anything,' she replied. 'I simply told him the truth. I don't trust the man, and for all I know he could be planning on killing me too.'

'And if I go with you then he could just be planning on making it three.'

'I suppose that's a possibility, Arthur, yes.'

I chuckled despite myself. 'You don't sound as though you're overly concerned by the prospect.'

'I'd certainly feel a lot safer if you came with me.'

'You sound like you have faith in me.'

'Right now you're the only person I can turn to,' she said. 'Besides, I'm sure you're used to this sort of thing and will know how to get us all through it if anyone can.'

'You've gone quiet, Arthur,' she said, her voice gone all husky and full of honey and smoke.

'I was thinking.'

'What were you thinking about?'

'Lots of things.'

'Was I one of those things?'

'You were lots of them, babe.'

32

She let out a sort of snort that I figured must pass for a laugh in her language. 'Take the Rembrandt home with you,' she said, 'and wait for my call.'

'You're sure they don't know where I live?'

'How could they?'

'All right.'

'You don't sound very convinced, Arthur. Don't you trust me?'

I let that one go sailing by. 'You've gone quiet on me again, Arthur.'

'I said all right, didn't I?'

'There's no need to be like that.'

'I'm not being like anything.'

'So you'll go home and wait for my call, with the Rembrandt, then?'

'I said all right.'

'All I want is to get Gisela back,' she said.

'Well you should have her back before the day's over.'

'Let's hope so. I'm so anxious and worried for her right now I can hardly stand it.'

'Worrying about her won't get you anywhere.'

'I know you're right, Arthur, but I just can't help it.'

We both went quiet again.

'I can trust in you, Arthur, can't I?'

'What's the matter?' I said. 'You think I'm going to run off to Brazil with your precious Rembrandt?'

'No, but–'

'But what?'

'Some people would.'

'Yeah, well some people might do a lot of things, but I'm not them.'

'I don't think you are, Arthur, either,' she said. 'I didn't think you were the first time I set eyes on you. I just had this feeling about you, right away, you know?'

'What sort of feeling was that?'

'Oh, that you were nice and honest and straight down the line.' She paused a moment and then went on: 'You've got that nice old-fashioned way about you that some Englishmen have. I spotted that about you right away.'

'You sound as though you like the English, Inge.'

'I've always had a soft spot for them, if I'm honest,' she confessed. 'There's something wonderfully sincere and… well, straight about them.'

'Straight?' I replied. 'That's a good word.'

'I'm using it in the old-fashioned sense of course.'

'It's funny,' I said, 'but I'd always got the impression you Germans didn't like us Brits very much.'

'What on earth gave you that idea, Arthur?'

'Oh I don't know, just the little matter of those two wars you waged against us, I suppose.'

'You shouldn't let that sort of thing mislead you.'

'No?'

'That was just politics, after all.'

155

33

'You almost make it sound like you had me down for the kind of guy a girl wouldn't mind taking home for tea,' I said.

'That's exactly what I meant, Arthur.'

'You mean you're going to invite me to meet Mutter?'

'She's dead, unfortunately.'

'I'm sorry.'

'Don't be... you didn't kill her, after all.'

I wished I'd never brought up the idea of having her take me to meet her mother in the first place. It had been a stupid thing to say. Some charmer I was turning out to be, I thought.

She said, 'I'd be happy to invite you to tea, though, when this is all over.'

'With scones and cream and fresh strawberries?'

'I know just the place.'

I laughed.

'What's so funny?'

'Nothing.'

'Well something must be.'

'This is hardly the place to enjoy high tea,' I said.

'No, but you can get it if you know where to go.'

'Like most things, I suppose,' I said. 'Why, you can even find a Rembrandt here, if you look hard enough. And I should know.'

She didn't say anything.

'How did you get it, anyway?' I asked.

'I thought I told you.'

'Perhaps you wouldn't mind running it by me again?'

'I inherited it from my father.'

'And he's dead, too, I take it?'

'Yes.'

'So how did Papa come by a Rembrandt?'

'I suppose he must've bought it.'

'You suppose?'

'I never asked him.'

'There can't be that many of them floating around in this part of the world, I shouldn't've thought.'

'I really wouldn't know.'

'You're sure it's an original Rembrandt and not a fake?'

'Of course.'

'What makes you so sure?'

'Father had it checked by experts.'

'So the kidnappers must've found out that you'd inherited it.'

'I guess so.'

We both went quiet again. In the distance, away to my right, I could see an eagle circling high up in the sky. I wondered if it was the same one I'd seen earlier, on my way up here. It must be on the lookout for prey.

Just then, I saw a huge boulder come bounding down the rock face. It was heading straight into my path. I jerked the wheel hard to the left to try to avoid hitting it, and that's the last thing I remember before my car crashed into the roadside.

At least I had the good sense to steer away from the edge, because if I'd steered the other way I'd have been a goner. And so would the Rembrandt.

34

It took me a few seconds to work out where I was when I opened my eyes. Then I realized I was at home, and in my own bed. But how had I got here? I was confused. The last thing I could recall, I was driving my car. It was hot and my shirt was wet with sweat. Away in the distance, an eagle was wheeling through the sky, high up, lording it over all below like some ancient country squire of the skies. I was on the phone, talking. To Inge. Yes, that's it. I was talking to Inge. I had to make a real effort to try to think in a logical fashion. I told myself that I wasn't in my car any more. I was in bed. In my own bed, at home. Yes, I'd already established that. Had I been drunk? No. I'd been driving and I was perfectly *compos mentis*. But what about after that? What happened after I stopped talking to Inge on my mobile? Ah yes. The rock fell into my path. Yes. I'd crashed. Yes. Not that I remembered the crash itself. That was all a blank. Just the rock falling. I recalled seeing it coming down the cliff face. Recalled the feeling I had when I saw it. Recalled thinking, Oh my God, it's going to hit me. Recalled steering hard to the left. That was lucky. If I'd gone the other way, I'd have gone over the edge. I must have crashed into something. I think I may still have been suffering with concussion, because I couldn't remember a thing after that. I moved my toes, just to check they were all in place. They were. I bent my knee. That was still there, too. And it bent okay. As for the other knee, it hurt, which must mean that it was still there, too. I figured I must have hurt it in the crash. It moved, though, when I asked it to, although it did need a little coaxing. I wriggled my fingers. Everything seemed to be in place. So far, so good. But how did I get in bed, then? And how come I wasn't in a hospital? Somebody must have brought me home. And seeing as I didn't have any clothes on, except for my pants, I figured somebody must have undressed me and put me in bed. Who, though? I had no idea. I must have been knocked out in the crash, because everything after that was a blank.

I heard voices. There were people in the flat. Who? I wondered. I swung a leg over the side of the bed. That doesn't sound like a particularly difficult operation to perform, but it all depends on the circumstances, and on this occasion it cost me some, I can tell you. Next I swung my other leg over. That one proved to be easier to move. Now all I had to do was stand up. I heard the voices again. Who the hell was out there? The people who brought me here, I supposed. They'd be ambulance men, then, maybe a nurse or a doctor. But why had they brought me home instead of taking me to a hospital? Or had I been in a hospital and forgotten I'd been there?

I figured I'd better go and investigate, see who it was that was out there. I pushed myself up off the mattress and just hoped that my body obeyed the commands I was giving it. It did, by and large. Enough to get me up on my feet, anyway. I was feeling kind of lightheaded and weak, but I was standing. Looking down, I realized that I was naked apart from my underpants. What the hell, I thought, and took a step. It felt a little like walking on the moon. Not that I've ever been up there and given it a go, but if I ever do get the chance to go there for a holiday then I reckon walking on it would feel pretty much like I was feeling right then.

Just then, the door opened. My oh my. Who should it be but my old friend Salvador Cobos. Only he hadn't been so friendly to me of late. 'What are you doing here?' I said.

Sal threw me a look that was about as warm as a wet mackerel. 'I was about to ask you the same thing, Arthur.'

'It may have escaped your attention, Sal, but it's my bedroom we're in.'

'It hasn't escaped my attention, Arthur. I'm pretty observant that way.'

'Glad to hear it,' I said. 'It speaks volumes for your powers of observation. I just thought I'd mention it in case.'

He looked me up and down. 'Might be an idea if you were to put some clothes on.'

'It might,' I agreed.

Looking around the room, I saw that my clothes had been left in the chair over in the corner. I did my moonwalk over to said chair, and I can tell you that I didn't resemble Michael Jackson the slightest bit while I was about it.

'You're looking a little out of it, Arthur.'

'That's not so bad.'

'What do you mean by that?'

'If I only look a *little bit* out of it, I mean…because I feel *one helluva lot* out of it.'

'I was using understatement.'

'Irony, you mean?'

'If you'd like to call it that.'

'I thought irony was my line.'

'Must be catching,' Sal said.

'Clearly is.' I was having a fight with a pair of socks. They were only a dinky little pair of black things, but they were giving me no end of trouble. I was trying to get them acquainted with my toes and they were having none of it. I had the feeling we could go on like this all day, my recalcitrant socks, my toes and me.

'Like watching a game of chess,' Sal Cobos observed.

'What is?'

'Never mind,' he said. 'Perhaps it might help if you were to sit on the bed while you do that.'

'Perhaps it might,' I agreed.

I sat on the bed and had another go.

'You want some help?'

'That would be cheating,' I said.

He gave me a straight look. 'You been drinking, Arthur?'

'Nope.'

'What, then?'

'I was in a car crash,' I explained, 'and now I'm trying to play chess with a pair of socks … If I can only move my rook to pawn four then it should free my little toe up with any luck.'

'Very funny.'

'You started it.'

'Perhaps you won't find it so funny if I tell you that you're under arrest.'

'Me?'

'Nobody else but us in this room, Arthur.'

'Since when's it been illegal to play chess with a pair of socks?'

'I'm not arresting you for that.'

'What, then?'

'Try and think back, Arthur.'

'Already tried that.'

'Try harder.'

I had another go, then shook my head. 'I already told you,' I said. 'I crashed the car and that's all I remember.'

'Was the girl in the car with you at the time?'

'What girl?'

'Come on, Arthur, don't try and get cute with me.'

'I'm not trying to do anything except put my socks on, Sal.'

'You're always trying to get cute, Arthur. It's the way you are.' Sal Cobos sighed. 'Think you're a cut above, don't you?'

'Do I?'

'Course you do,' he said, rolling the product of his excavations between forefinger and thumb. 'Think you're too good to wear a uniform, that it? See yourself as that English detective, no doubt. Sherlock Homes, do you?'

'Holmes,' I corrected him.

'*Eso es.*' He nodded. 'That's what I said. Sherlock Homes.'

35

'What's Sherlock Holmes got to do with anything?'

'The lone genius who solves the case single handed, but not before he's tied the local gendarmerie up in knots along the way.'

'The gendarmerie are French,' I said, 'and Sherlock Holmes was English.'

'Same difference.' He shrugged. 'Gendarmerie. Policia. Polizei. Police. All means the same.'

'They call them bobbies in English.'

'If I ever want EFL lessons, Arthur, I'll be sure to drop you a line.'

I turned my attention back to my recalcitrant toes.

'Isn't it about time you grew up, Arthur?'

'Isn't it about time you got to the point, Sal?'

'I'm getting there.'

'What's that you were saying about a girl?'

'Yes, the girl… Was she in the car when you crashed, Arthur?'

'No, she wasn't.'

'So you picked her up afterwards, then?'

'Maybe she picked me up.'

'You mean she was flirting with you, is that what you're saying?' he said. 'Do you mean to say that you knew this girl from before, Arthur?'

'What girl would this be, Sal?'

'The one that you said flirted with you.'

'I never said any girl flirted with me.'

'But you just said it.'

'No, it was you that said it, Sal. I was just trying to follow your train of thought, and finding it a little tricky to do so, I must admit.'

'It's not going to do you any good, Arthur, getting clever like this.'

'Since when's it been an offence to be clever in this part of the world?'

'Look,' he said, 'your goose is cooked, so you might as well play ball now. It's the only thing to do in a situation like yours. What do you say?'

'What situation would that be, Sal? Are we talking about my not being able to get my socks on, and you watching me not being able to do it?'

'We're talking about the girl you killed, Arthur.'

'The girl, I *what*…?'

'You heard.'

'I didn't kill anybody.'

'Where did you pick her up, Arthur?'

'What girl are you talking about?'

'You said you knew her from beforehand, right?'

'No, wrong.'

'So how come she was flirting with you, then? Where did you meet her?'

'Where did I meet who?'

'The girl, you idiot. Are you drunk or something?'

'I think I may be a little concussed.'

'That figures.'

'After the accident,' I said.

'So you killed her before and put her in the car, is that it?'

'You keep talking to me about this girl, Sal,' I said, 'but I don't know who you mean.'

'Oh I think you do, Arthur.'

'What girl are you talking about?'

'The one you killed.'

'Which girl am I supposed to have killed?'

'The one who's lying on the carpet in the front room.'

'In the front room...?'

'That's right,' Cobos said. 'At least she was in there the last time I looked, just before I came in here. And she sure didn't look like she was about to go anywhere. Been murdered. Strangled, to be precise. And in my experience, Arthur, girls who've been strangled don't generally get up off the floor and leave a place. I mean, I know you might think I'm a dumb cop and all, but even I know that much.'

I could hear the words that Salvador Cobos was saying, but I was having difficulty making any sense of them. This girl, he said, where did I pick her up? Maybe she was flirting with me. Had I known her from before? This girl who was lying on the carpet?

Wait a moment. On *the carpet, did he say? Yes, on the carpet? On my carpet? None other. In the front room,* he'd said. The carpet. The one with the floral pattern. Only he didn't say that about the floral pattern. That's me thinking. That's me, trying to make sense. *Strangled.* He'd said she'd been strangled. Girls who've been strangled aren't in the habit of getting up and walking out of a place, he said. Well he was right there. It was starting to come to me. I was starting to piece it together, what he'd been saying. Starting to take the words and see how he'd connected them up. But they couldn't mean what I thought they meant. No. Sal Cobos couldn't have said what I thought he'd said. I was concussed. It was after the crash. The rock came down the cliff face, you know. Oh yes. I steered hard to the left. Good choice, that. Right was no good. Steer right and I'd have been a goner. Good night, Irene. Don't call me, and I won't call you. On the carpet, he'd said. The strangled girl. He couldn't mean that. No. He couldn't have said that. He said I was trying to play a game of chess with my socks. That was funny. He was being ironic. Not his usual style. He was learning from me. My pinky was the rook, the next toe was my knight, the middle one was the bishop; the next was the queen, then the king. Or did I say that about playing chess? So where did the sock come into it? And what about the girl? And who strangled her? And what was she doing on my carpet, in my front room? There was something about my front room lately. That journalist guy had wound up dead in there, too. On the sofa. Fontana. Somebody Fontana. Javier. Worked for *La Vanguarda*. Came all the way down here from Figarillo, to talk to me. How was it that people seemed to end up dying around me?

Just then, the sock slipped all the way up my foot. Check mate, I thought. Wait a moment, I thought. What was that about a girl again? Did I dream all that, or was it for real?

I looked at Sal Cobos, just to check he was really Sal Cobos and not just a Sal Cobos I was dreaming about. He was the real Sal Cobos, all right.

I said, 'What's been going on, Sal?'

He cocked a grey-flecked brow, and looked at me like he was trying to make out whether or not I was for real; then he said, 'That's what I need you to tell me, Arthur.'

36

So they took me down to the Jefatura and threw me in a cell. It was nothing new to me, but even so I didn't feel good about being in there. Who does? The walls were stained with blood and excrement, as were the mattress and blanket.

I banged on the bars of my cell and invoked my right to speak to my lawyer in raucous terms and tones. The guard on duty outside employed similarly raucous terms and tones to tell me to shut the fuck up. So much for my human rights, I shouted back. The guard came over and peered in at me through the bars of my cell. He told me they didn't 'do' human rights here. I wanted comfort and luxury, I could go check out the Hilton. Except I couldn't right now because I was banged up. Very funny. But of course we did, I replied. Bardino was in Europe, after all. The guard begged to differ. I suggested he go take a look at a map. He suggested I go take a flying fuck at my mattress.

But in fairness it wasn't too long before the door opened and my lawyer, Carmen Gordano, was shown in. Truth is, I heard her coming. You can always hear Carmen coming. It's part of her style. Carmen has always struck me as something of a cross between Uma Thurman and Cruella Deville. I mean, she's tall and she's got these cheekbones and shoulders and legs. Today she was wearing a grey shark's tooth jacket with a matching skirt and a silk shirt and she looked uncompromisingly, indeed almost violently professional, which is to say just the way you'd want your lawyer to look if you were in trouble.

She looked at me like she'd already decided she was going to hit me and was trying to make up her mind whether to go for my glass chin or my even glassier balls. Carmen always looks at me like this when I'm in trouble. It's her way. Then she cracks this grin that she has. It's her way of letting me know that she's going to forgive me just this one more time. Never mind that she's already started charging me an hourly rate that is criminally exorbitant, right from the time she was called, and the clock is ticking. I do mind this, of course. Who wouldn't? But I know better than to let it show. I cracked a smile. It wasn't much of a smile, but it was the best I could muster in the circumstances. 'Glad you could make it, Carmen,' I said.

'I gotta get you out,' she replied, 'if it's only for the laughs. You're too cute to be locked up inside, have your ass pronged by some primate.'

'I'm so glad you appreciate my ass, Carmen.'

'So what've you been up to this time?'

'It's a long story.'

'I'm listening.'

I ran it by her, cutting the story down to the bone.

'You really *are* getting to be a magnet for corpses, Arthur,' she said after she'd heard me out. 'What's got into you lately?'

'Ask not what I'm doing following corpses, but what the corpses are doing following me.'

'Have you got into voodoo or something?'

'My ex reckoned I was capable of working magic in the sack,' I said, 'but that's about as far as it goes.'

'Uh-uh,' Carmen nodded. 'That why she left you?'

I grinned and figured I'd better take the Fifth on that one, even though I wasn't a Yank.

'You know either of the two birds that got dead in your flat?'

'Nope. Never seen them before.'

'Mm...well if you want me to get you out of this one then you're expecting a miracle, you do know that?'

'What I've got you as my lawyer for, Carmen.'

'Yeah,' she said, 'well it's going to cost you. Miracles don't come cheap, you know.'

I shrugged and she had me sit down with her and go through everything that had happened, or as much as I could remember. When I'd finished telling her, she gave me a straight look and asked me if I really expected her to believe the story I'd just told her. I said that I did. 'It's the truth, after all,' I said.

She continued to look at me, long and hard. 'The truth, huh?'

'I'm being framed by someone.'

'Tell me a little more about the client you're working for.'

I told her that my client had hired me to find her sister, who'd gone missing; but I didn't reveal her identity. Carmen asked me to name her. I shook my head. 'Oh come on, Arthur. Your ass is on the line here.'

'You know me, Carmen. It's the way I work.'

'Carry on the way you're going and you won't be working much longer.'

'I've told you everything that I can,' I said. 'Besides, what does it matter who my client is? Her identity's not relevant... I mean I'm not in here because of her.'

'So it's a girl, then.'

'I never said that.'

'You said it was a *her*, and most hers are female in my experience.'

'You just haven't been around as much as I thought, Carmen.'

'You mean it's a shemale you're working for, a lady boy, or what...?'

'No, I was just joking.'

'This is no time to joke, Arthur, if you value your ass.'

'I value it.'

'Yes, but how much do you value it?'

'Okay,' I said, 'why don't you take what I've given you and see how far you can get with it?'

'You haven't give me much.'

'I've told you everything I know.'

'Two people have wound up dead in your living room, Arthur, in the past few days, and you're saying you don't know anything about it.'

'That's right.'

'You're bullshitting.'

'I'm telling you the truth, Carmen.'

'You wouldn't know the truth, Arthur, if it snuck up and bit you where it hurts.'

'It's already bitten me there,' I said. 'And I've got the marks to prove it.'

Carmen took a deep breath, battened her eyelids and breathed a little fire down her nostrils. 'What about this gangster character?'

'What about him?'

'He hung you in a pool with a shark in it, you said?'

'That's right.'

'What's he got against you?'

'I told you, I got in a fight with him.'

'Even so, I mean that's an extreme reaction, isn't it?'

'The man's an extreme character,' I said. 'I mean he's a psycho. The sort of guy just smiling at him could get you killed.'

'Sure sounds it.' She took a moment to reflect. 'Do you think he could be behind this?'

'It's possible, I guess.'

'Have you got any proof that this guy abducted you?'

'It was in the newspaper.'

'So people saw you fighting him, and then saw you being driven away in his car?'

'Yeah.'

'Well that's something,' she said. 'But we need to connect this Sharky character to the two bodies.'

I nodded. The man in the next cell had begun to yell his head off. He was saying something about his being a gypsy and not being able to stand it being locked up.

Should've thought of that when you stole the car, the officer on guard outside shouted back at him. The gypsy wanted to know how else he was going to support his heroin habit. The guard told him he should have considered all this before he started using. I had the feeling those two sweethearts were capable of going on in that way all through the evening, just like some married couples I know.

Carmen produced a pack of Camels from her Gucci handbag and lit up. She drew on it like it meant something to her. '*Por cojones*, Arthur,' she said. 'How did you manage to fuck up like this?'

I shrugged and said, 'I didn't do anything to make it happen.'

'Seems to me that there're two possible causes of all this.'

'Which are?'

'Either somebody hates you real bad and's out to get you.'

'Or?'

'You're bullshitting.'

'And I'm not bullshitting,' I said. 'I already told you that.'

'That's right. You did.'

She didn't seem like she was totally convinced.

'You do believe me, right?'

'I guess so.'

'I've never lied to you in the past, Carmen.'

'There's always a first time for everything, Arthur.'

'Well this ain't it.'

'Okay,' she said. 'I'll do my best for you, but I can't promise anything.'

It sounded pretty bad. But then, it *was* pretty bad. In fact, it was worse than that.

The door to the cell opened and two guards came in. One of them had a belly, the other didn't. The one with the belly said it was time for me to go up to the Interview room, so Carmen dropped her cigarette and stamped it out, then we went up with the guards.

37

Sal Cobos was sitting at the desk waiting for us when we entered the Interview room. He was wearing a grey suit, a white shirt, the top two buttons of which he'd left undone, and the kind of expression you might have expected to find on the mug of someone like Al Capone while he was planning the St Valentine's Day Massacre. 'Glad you could make it, Arthur,' he said. 'Why don't you come in and make yourself comfortable.'

Carmen and I sat on the two upright chairs that had been set out for us. They didn't make us feel at all comfortable; but then, I got the impression they weren't there for that purpose. Carmen fixed Sal Cobos with a feisty look and said, 'My client could do without being ridiculed, Inspector Jefe.'

'Just being friendly and trying to put him at his ease,' Cobos said. 'Anyway, your client and I know each other, don't we, Arthur?'

'That's no excuse. I refuse to allow you to intimidate my client.'

'Intimidating Arthur was the last thing on my mind, I can assure you. Besides, Arthur's not the kinda guy it's easy to intimidate.'

'You're making unfair assumptions about my client.'

'Okay, okay.' Cobos showed her a clean pair of palms. 'Let's just cut to the chase, shall we?'

'By all means.'

Cobos pushed a button to set the tape rolling. He said the date into the mic, then gave the names of all present and said where we were. 'Fact is,' he said, 'as you and your lawyer will recall from the last time we convened here to discuss recent events in your life, we had a call to say we could expect to find a journalist by the name of Javier Fontana at your place, Arthur.'

'And you didn't find him there.'

'No, we didn't... but he did show up dead the same day.'

'Sorry to hear about that.'

'Sure you are, Arthur.'

Carmen Gordano said, 'The fact that somebody's called you up to say a body can be found at my client's residence cannot be used against him, as the body wasn't found there.'

'No, that's true... but another body was, wasn't it, Arthur?'

'If you say so, Sal.'

'I do say so, Arthur. And the reason I say so is that the body *was found there*. A woman by the name of Gisela Schwartz. Strangled to death. What have you got to say about that, Arthur?'

I kept mum.

'Maybe I'm a little deaf, but I didn't quite catch what you said.'

'I don't make anything of it.'

'The girl was lying dead on your sofa when we arrived.'

Carmen Gordano said, 'What made you think you would find her there?'

'We had a tip off.'

'Thereby hangs a tale,' I said.

'What does that mean?'

'What you think it means.'

'I don't think it means anything.'

'Sure you do, Sal. You just want to act like you aren't thinking it.'

'Since when you been working as a shrink, Arthur?'

'I haven't.'

'So can we cut the amateur psychiatry bullshit?'

'It isn't bullshit.'

Carmen Gordano said, 'My client was merely quoting Shakespeare.'

'Was he now?'

'The English poet and playwright.'

'I know who Shakespeare is... Now can you please stop trying to sidetrack me?'

Carmen said, 'I object to the accusation that you have just made against my client.'

'Do you now?'

'I most certainly do. My client is cooperating with you, or at least he is trying to, despite your persistent attempts to intimidate and bully him.'

Sal Cobos took a deep breath. 'With all due respect, I'm trying to get at the truth.'

'So am I,' I said. 'I think you already know that, Sal. I want to catch the bad guys, too, and I've got a long history of catching them.'

'So?'

'So you know as well as I do that I've not killed anyone, so what's with all this bullshit?'

'I'm afraid I don't know any such thing, Arthur.'

'If you don't know it then you ought to.'

Sal Cobos leaned back in his chair and tented his fingers on his belly. His eyes narrowed to slits and his lips disappeared. 'All I know for sure, Arthur,' he said, 'is the facts. And the facts are that Gisela Schwartz got dead in your place. And I also strongly suspect that Javier Fontano called into your place to breathe his last, too.'

'What you've just said about this Fontana guy is pure supposition,' I replied. 'It's fiction, in fact. In so far as the girl is concerned, I wouldn't mind betting she got dead someplace else first and was then carried to my place and dumped there while I was unconscious.'

'You got anything to back up that assertion with?'

'The person or persons who tipped you off killed her, Sal. That's why they called you–to frame me. It's so obvious a child could see it.'

Inspector Jefe Salvador Cobos balled his fists and sprang up from his chair. 'You've got some balls to be talking to me like that, Arthur Blakey.'

Carmen said, 'I really must object to the violent, intimidating and distinctly inappropriate and unprofessional tone you are using in this interview, Inspector Jefe.'

'Listen to the two of you,' Cobos said. 'I can end this interview now and charge Arthur with murder in the first degree if that's the way you want it. And I can do it if it's not the way you want it, too. I'm only trying to give Arthur here the chance to play ball.'

'But my client *is* playing ball, Inspector Jefe,' Carmen replied, in tones you could have cut your steak with. 'With all due respect, Inspector, it's *you* who isn't.'

'What he means,' I said, 'is that he wants me to confess to the murder. That's what he'd call *playing ball.*'

'To both murders,' Cobos corrected me.

'But my client is hardly about to confess to a crime or crimes that he didn't commit,' Carmen snapped.

'It'll go easier on him if he does, and you both know it.'

'I didn't do it, Sal.'

'I know.' He shook his head and let out a sigh that also let us know just how

fed up with me he was. 'You didn't do it and you don't know nothing, Arthur, is that it?'

'That's it.'

'It's way too late to be taking that line with me,' he said. 'I mean, I want to help you here, don't you understand?'

I said, 'I thought you said you were after the truth?'

'I am.'

'In that case I've told you everything I know.'

'There's something you're not telling me,' Cobos objected. 'Either you killed the two victims or you're covering for someone. Whichever it is, you're going down if you don't open up and tell me what you know. I need you to give me something, and whatever it is it'd better be good because this is your last chance, Arthur.'

At that moment, the door opened and a plainclothes officer–five-ten, lean, short brown hair, black jeans and short-sleeved white shirt–entered the room. Without looking at me or Carmen Gordano, he came over to the table and whispered something in Sal Cobos's ear. Sal nodded slowly when he heard what the guy had to say, and he bit his lip and frowned. It looked like whatever it was he'd just heard had given him plenty to think about. And he didn't seem to be enjoying the process, either, judging from his expression. His eyes peered out at me through their curtained lids with a smoky ferocity. If he could have sentenced me to a stint of spontaneous combustion there and then, I'd have been nothing more than so much smoke and dust.

'Is that all?' I asked.

'Yes, it is.'

I'd hardly been expecting to hear him say that. 'You mean that I can go?'

'Yes, you're free to leave.'

I stayed where I was, as if gummed to my chair.

Cobos said, 'Didn't you hear what I just said? You're free to go.'

'What's it all about?' I asked.

Carmen was on her feet. 'Come on, Arthur,' she said. 'Let's get out of this place. You heard what the man said. You can buy me a glass of Chablis someplace.'

I was too curious to leave my chair right away, or to take my eyes off Inspector Jefe Sal Cobos. 'But what did that man say to you when he came in a moment ago, Sal?'

'It really is ironic, do you know that?' He mustered a sour grin. 'You go to all these lengths to keep your client's identity a secret, even allowing yourself to be banged up and face being charged with murder, and then she just comes waltzing in here and spills the beans.'

'Who does?'

'Why your client, of course—Inge Schwartz.'

'What did she say?'

'She said that you're not the man who killed her sister, for a start.'

'That was nice of her.'

'You think she was only saying it because she likes you?'

'No.'

'Because if she was lying then you can tell me, Arthur.'

'No, she was telling you the truth, Sal.'

'But you sounded surprised.'

I shrugged. 'Just because a thing's true, it doesn't mean you can't sometimes be surprised when you hear that someone's told it like it is.'

'You don't exactly sound as though you trust your client, Arthur.'

'I didn't say that.'

'Just a cynic by nature, that it?'

'What else did she tell you?'

'That she employed you to look for her sister who'd been kidnapped, and that you'd been hit on the head. She reckoned the kidnapper or kidnappers must've killed her sister someplace else first, then broken into your flat and put her on the sofa there. She says you were with her all evening, and seeing as we know that the time of death was last evening it seems like you're probably in the clear for the time being.'

'For the *time being*?'

'That's right,' Cobos said. 'The woman could be lying, so you're still a suspect, but I've decided not to arrest yet.'

'Did my client tell you who kidnapped her sister?'

Sal Cobos shook his head. 'Said she didn't know…that's why she employed you, right?–to try'n find out.'

'That's right.'

'But you didn't find out, did you, Arthur?'

'No, I didn't, Sal.'

'Mm…well either that makes you a liar or a private dick who failed to get his man.'

'It makes me the latter.'

'Which ain't good, Arthur.'

'No, good it sure isn't, Sal, but it's better than being a liar.'

'I'd agree with you there.'

I got up and made for the door. Carmen followed me. Just as we were about to go out, Sal said, 'Arthur, if you ever find out who did kidnap Gisela Schwartz you will tell me, right?'

'You're the first person I'll call, Sal,' I said, and with that Carmen and I left the Jefatura.

It was good to be out in the street again. It was hot and sunny still, despite the fact that it was coming up to 9 p.m., and I was a free man once more. Things could have been a lot worse. I turned to Carmen and said, 'Seems like I got lucky.'

'Seems like you did, Arthur.'

38

As I walked something kept gnawing at my conscience. I felt like I'd screwed up and owed Inge big time. Not only had I lost her priceless Rembrandt original but I'd also failed to find her sister Gisela–until the poor girl had shown up dead on my sofa of all places. Then Inge had taken pity on me and got me out of jail, after everything I'd done–or failed to do, rather.

I figured the least I could do was return the fee I'd charged her. I called her number several times, but she didn't pick up. I figured she must be angry with me all right. Not that I could blame her.

Having reached the building where I live, I went in and started up the stairs. I was so tired by now that my feet felt like lumps of lead. I reached into my pocket and brought out the door key as I headed along the landing, and I'd just put it into the lock when I heard something–or some*body*–move behind me. I turned and found myself looking at Inge Schwartz.

'It's you,' I said.

'Who did you expect, the Boston Strangler?'

'Not exactly... he's been dead for years.' She took a step towards me. 'Look, I wanted to give you back the fee I charged you.'

'That's very gallant of you,' she said. 'Maybe somebody ought to tell you that nobody returns fees they've earned nowadays. That sort of thing went out with Philip Marlowe.'

'Inge, I screwed up big time and I feel bad about it.'

'Don't bust your balls crying over spilt milk, mister.'

'Was that all your sister was to you—spilt milk?'

'I loved Gisela, but now she's gone. And beating yourself up about it's not going to bring her back.' She let out a heavy sigh. 'Besides, you didn't kill her, even if you're talking like you think you did. On the contrary, you did everything you could to try to find her.'

'Then there's your Rembrandt.'

'Yeah, well I wanted to talk to you about that. Maybe if you'd like to invite me in?'

'Sure,' I said. 'Be my guest.' I turned and opened the door, then held it for her before I followed her into the flat.

'Make yourself comfortable.'

'I'm not in that kind of mood, Arthur.' She stood very close to me there just inside the doorway, next to the coat stand, and the irises of her eyes were blue as the sea. 'I think you're honest, Arthur, and that's a quality I value in a man.' Her voice was throaty and husky, full of smoke and honey.

'If you're trying to massage my wounded male ego then you needn't bother.'

'Do you expect me to say sorry to you, after everything that's happened, Arthur?'

'No.'

'What then?'

'Oh I don't know.' I could smell her jasmine scent and it was playing jazzy scales up and down my spinal cord. I took her in my arms and kissed her on the mouth. When I finally came up for air, she buried her face in my lapel and began to sob. I ran my hand through her hair and said, 'Inge…' That was all I could manage. She straightened up and dabbed at the corners of her eyes with a small handkerchief she'd produced from her pocket, then she said, 'I need you to find the man who killed my sister.'

'I'm not sure I can do that.'

'But you can at least try, can't you?'

'Okay,' I said. 'I'll give it my best shot.' I reckoned it was the least I could do.

'And if you happen to turn up the Rembrandt while you're at it then I'll pay you well for your trouble.'

'I'll only charge you my usual fee plus expenses.'

'But I insist on offering you a little commission, Arthur.'

'I can't take it. If I do find the Rembrandt then I'll only be getting back what I lost, is the way I see it.'

'You didn't lose it exactly, though—rocks fell into your path. You might have been killed.'

'You paid me to deliver the Rembrandt over as ransom, and I failed to do.'

'But has it occurred to you that the kidnapper didn't want you to deliver it?' she replied. 'I mean, it had to be him who took it.'

'That possibility had occurred to me, yes.'

'The way I see it, Arthur, it's more than just a possibility.'

'Maybe you're right,' I said. 'And if you are then the kidnapper never had any intention of handing Gisela over alive.'

'Exactly.'

'What I'm wondering is how he found out where I was.'

'I have no idea, Arthur. You're the detective, you tell me.' Inge reached into the rose-coloured jacket she was wearing and brought out her purse, opened it and took out a wad of fifties. 'Here,' she said, 'this should keep you going.'

I took the clump of money and looked at it. I had no idea how much was there, but it was certainly a tidy sum and much more than I felt I had earned. 'Keep it,' I said.

'No, I want you to have it, Arthur. You're a pro, right?'

'I like to think so.'

'So act like one,' she said. 'And you can start by putting the money I just gave you into your wallet. I don't like to work with amateurs. They give me the willies.'

I did as she said. As I was putting my wallet away, she made for the door. 'I'll be in touch,' she said, 'and good luck.' With that, she opened the door and went out.

So I was back on the case. Not that I'd ever really left it.

39

Right now I had about as much juice left in me as a bunch of dried out grapes, and I felt like all my pips had been surgically extracted. I found the bottle of Scotch and poured myself a large one, then sat in the easy chair and did some hard thinking about the case. I wondered how the kidnapper had found out who and where I was.

Of course Inge had told him she would be bringing me along to swap the Rembrandt for her sister, Gisela, but she hadn't mentioned my name. She'd just said that I was a friend of the family. Obviously the kidnapper hadn't bought her story and had done a little digging around of his own. Whoever he was, the guy was clearly one step ahead of Inge and me.

I took a drive down to the morgue and spoke to Pedro Morante, the doctor who'd performed the autopsy. Morante's medium height and build and was wearing green chinos with yachting loafers and a short-sleeved shirt. He's in his mid-forties and has a calm and methodical manner. I treated him to breakfast in the local café, and he told me what he knew about Gisela Schwartz and the manner of her death. He began by telling me she'd been a fine specimen of womanhood, and what a shame it was when a beautiful young girl like that gets killed. Then he told me that Gisela Schwartz had died as a result of asphyxiation due to strangulation. Forensics had not found any foreign prints or DNA of any kind on the body. He realized that the body had been found on the sofa at my place, but there was nothing to suggest I had killed her—beyond the circumstantial evidence inherent in the fact he'd just described. I was pleased to note this, but assured him I'd never had any reason to fear the contrary might be the case, given that I had not in fact killed the woman. I had been hired to try to find the girl, I explained. Well I'd sure done that, Morante said. That I had, I agreed, although sadly I'd arrived on the scene a little too late. Ideally I should like to have found her *before* she was killed. Ideally that would indeed have been a better outcome all round, the doctor agreed. He was very calm and methodical in his speech, as he was in his manner of eating and drinking. Watching him bite into his ham roll, I half expected him to take it apart first and give its constituent parts a thorough inspection. He didn't, though. He merely chewed and gazed across the bar as if he were rather sad and bored by the way the day was turning out.

I finished my beer and paid the bill before I thanked Morante for his help and took my leave of him. I wondered what my next move ought to be as I walked back to my car. I still hadn't come up with an answer by the time I'd started up the ignition, so I just cruised around the streets of Bardino for a time and hoped that something would occur to me. The sun went down while I was driving and the lights came on, and I began to wonder about Vince Caportorio and what he got up to when he wasn't feeding people to his pet shark. Perhaps he was behind all this.

He was bad and mean enough for the job. Not only that, but he'd expressed a definite interest in ascertaining the whereabouts of the Rembrandt the last time our paths had crossed, so he had to be a prime candidate. In fact, right now he was the *only* candidate on my list.

I went and parked across the street from his bar and kept watch on the place, figuring he'd probably show sooner or later. I wasn't quite sure what I was going to do when he did, but I figured I'd think of something. I usually do.

I'd been waiting there for the best part of an hour when who else but Sal Cobos showed. He tapped on the window and when I buzzed it down he said, 'I thought I'd find you here, Arthur.' He sighed to add a little dramatic effect to what he had to say and went on: 'Anyone else, anyone with a head on their shoulders that's to say, would have enough sense to leave Vince Caportorio and his people well alone. But not you.'

'I suppose I just didn't get the proper kind of schooling.'

'That's not what I heard about you,' he replied. 'I was told you come from money.'

'I wouldn't go that far.'

'The rumour is the school you went to's about the poshest there is.'

I grinned at him and he asked what was so funny. 'I didn't figure you for the type to be impressed by that sort of thing.'

'I'm not, Arthur,' he said, 'and you can wipe that silly smile off your face.'

'I'm a happy sort of a guy, Sal.'

'You won't be for very long, if Vince and his mutts have another chance with you.'

'That's between me and Vince.'

'Yes, I suppose it is,' he agreed. 'But you might like to know that Vince is planning on spending a quiet night in with his ladylove.'

'What makes you so sure of that?'

'We've got men outside keeping an eye on his place, and he had his driver go and pick his girlfriend up earlier and take her to his. He only does that when he's not going out anywhere.'

I considered what Cobos had just told me for a short while; then I looked at him and said, 'How's the investigation into Gisela Schwartz's death going?'

'We've got a few interesting leads, Arthur.' He peered at me like I was something under a microscope. 'Thing is, most of them seem to lead to you.'

I figured this was my opportunity to come back with some witty riposte, but for once I was lost for words. Finally I said, 'I think you know that I didn't kill the girl or the reporter or those other two, Ribera and Gross, Sal.'

'I think what I always think where you're concerned, Arthur.'

'What's that?'

'You're not telling everything you know,' he said. 'And the stuff you're telling's not worth knowing.'

I glanced at my wristwatch. I was tired and Vince was having a night in, so there didn't seem to be much point in hanging around outside of his place. 'Oh well, Sal, I'd love to be able to sit and talk like this all evening,' I replied. 'But I've been working hard lately and sleep's been short on supply, so I think I'll call it a day.'

Sal said, 'Take care nobody breaks into your place and dies on your sofa while you're asleep tonight, Arthur.'

40

I dreamed that night that I was swimming in the sea. The tide was going out and I was heading back to the beach, and it was hard going. Then I spotted a fin sticking up out of the water, and my heart started to pound away in my chest. Maybe it's a dolphin, I thought, but I knew it was a shark. Then it began to come towards me. All I could see was the fin moving through the water very quickly. I figured my only chance was to try and punch it on the nose. Then I woke up with a start. I wondered where I was for a moment, and then, when I realized I was at home, I breathed a sigh of relief. I told myself I was a fool for dreaming about having a shark come after me, because everyone knew you didn't get sharks in the Med.

I was feeling clammy and thirsty, so I got up and went out into the kitchen, where I poured the tap and let it run a little. Then I filled a pint mug and drank it all down in one, before I went back to bed. But I lay there tossing and turning for what seemed like ages. My mind was too full of the case to let me sleep. How did the kidnapper know I had the Rembrandt when I went and retrieved it from the house in the village for Inge? Hadn't I taken great care to ensure that I wasn't being followed?

The same question kept going round in my mind, and I kept coming up with zilch for an answer. Then I figured it might be worth taking a drive back to the spot where I'd been when I last had the Rembrandt. I could remember the rocks coming down the mountainside into my path, and that was it. Everything was a blur after that. But maybe if I went back there, it might help me to recall what happened. It was a long shot, but right now all I had was long shots or no shots at all. And the former were better than the latter.

I looked at my wristwatch: 6.30 a.m. If I left now then it would be light by the time I'd got there. So I had a quick breakfast of toast with olive oil and coffee, then went and found my Porsche. It wasn't long before I'd left Bardino behind me and was climbing up into the mountains. I drove with the windows down, and the scent of the scorched land wafted in as I went along. Then I found myself looking down over the *pueblo* from above. It was like a jewel laid out on a bed of satin, and beyond was the large vast darkness of the Mediterranean.

I reckoned I could remember how to get to the village all right, so I gave my GPS a rest and drove from memory in the hope that it might help me to recall the day I'd gone there. And sure enough all sorts of memories began to come back to me as I drove. I remembered going into the house and finding the Rembrandt. I remembered leaving the house with it, and thinking everything was cool. Certainly I hadn't thought I was being followed. By now the sun had come up, but it was still quite cool, although I was sure it would be hot later in the morning. A road sign told me that I was just some eight kilometers from Magro. I was eager to get there, for some reason, even though I had no reason to be confident that I'd turn up anything worth a bean once I did. But that's the way I am. I tend to work on instinct a lot of the time. Sometimes my instincts are right and sometimes they're wrong, but I'd be nowhere at all without them. It's not the sort of stuff they teach them in the police academies nowadays, I know, but that's never bothered me. I thought of Inge Schwartz, and how beautiful she was. And how good holding her in my arms and kissing her the night before had made me feel. I realized that I'd been thinking about her in that way quite a bit of late. But what guy wouldn't get to thinking that way about a girl like her, if he knew her? I was only human, after all.

Then I came to the spot where I'd had the accident. If 'accident' is the right word, I thought. Because I still wasn't sure about that. It was what I'd come here to try and find out.

I pulled over and got out of the car. To my right, there was a small metal barrier where the road curved, and I found myself looking down on the ravine that lay in wait for the hapless driver. The barrier, which only stretched some four or five metres, had clearly taken a few knocks, which was hardly surprising because it was a sharp corner. Turning away and looking back up the road, I recalled driving along here. I recalled how hot it had been. Recalled seeing the rocks falling from the cliff face to my left, and then jerking the wheel to avoid crashing into the barrier and possibly through it and going on down to what would have been certain death in the ravine below. After that it was all a blank.

I crossed the road and a great stone boulder that jutted out of the rock face caught my attention. There seemed to be something familiar about it, and I concluded that it might well have been the last thing I'd seen before I crashed. Somebody must have been waiting for me on the side of the road, I thought. But I couldn't recall having seen anyone.

Or there was another possible explanation, which was that the person or persons who'd taken the Rembrandt hadn't been waiting for me at all, but rather had come to my aid in the first instance. Presuming that was what had happened, they could have set about trying to help me and then decided to rob me when they saw that I had a Rembrandt in my car. It was certainly true that times were hard over here right now, and nowhere was the pinch being felt more than in this part of the country, in the small mountain villages, where work was so scarce as to appear to be out of fashion. If this theory was correct, then whoever it was that found me might have seen me as easy pickings. Somebody from the city who drove a flash car and possessed all the things they wanted but had no way of acquiring. Could that have been what happened? I wondered.

It was possible, I supposed. Somehow I didn't fancy this idea, though. It seemed too haphazard, too much of a coincidence. And I've always hated coincidences. I've seen too many of them over the years that just haven't added up. Coincidences that ultimately turned out to be anything but; seemingly chance occurrences that long hours of toil finally led me to conclude were in fact part of a carefully conceived plan engendered by some ingenious criminal. And as if I'd needed any more confirmation where this theory of mine on coincidences was concerned, I only had to reflect on the habit of following me about that dead bodies seemed to have acquired lately.

I looked up above, half expecting to see a huge boulder come crashing down the slope towards me. But there was no sign of any loose rocks being about to fall upon me, or into my path, today. The question was, whether the rocks that caused me to crash had fallen, or whether they were given a helping hand.

I followed the road on round the corner. From there it climbed back on itself, and I walked on up until I was able to look down upon my car where I'd left it by the roadside. If someone had been waiting for me to come back along the road, ready to ambush me by hurtling rocks down the cliff face into my path, then this would have been the perfect spot for it. I pushed at a few of the boulders that were jutting out of the cliff face. They refused to move an inch, and I was sure an elephant couldn't have caused them to budge. Perhaps they brought some rocks with them in the back of a car or truck and offloaded them into my path, when they saw me coming along the road, I thought. Was that possible? Sure it was.

But presuming somebody had been up here waiting to ambush me, I was still no closer to discovering the person's identity.

The sun had definitely clocked on for work by now, and I was feeling its effects. From now on the day would just get hotter and hotter, and it would stay hot until sundown. It must be easy being a weatherman in this region. If only my own job were half as straightforward. I was angry and frustrated, because somebody had taken me for a fool. And whoever that somebody was, they had my client's Rembrandt and were no doubt looking to sell it. I reckoned that might not be such an easy thing to do, though, in these parts. The list of potential buyers would be severely limited by a number of factors, the way I saw it. For a start, few people had the kind of money the thief would want to sell it for. And presuming people did have that kind of money, then they were likely to be put off by the thought that they'd be buying stolen property. Popular myths with regard to art thefts being carried out to order for criminal billionaires were very often just that. And you couldn't very well go hawking a stolen Rembrandt around town.

These thoughts bucked me up a little, so that I began to feel that I might be down but I was not yet out. I wandered along the road, looking down over the ravine as I did so. I was on the lookout for something, only I didn't have any real idea as to what that something might be. So much of detective work is going through the motions, doing the things that you know you're supposed to do, and looking in the places you know you're supposed to look, and feeling all the while you're about it that you're most probably wasting your time; but you do it even so. You do it because you have to do something. You do it because you never know. Because just when you think you're never going to find something, you can sometimes chance upon a vital piece of evidence or information. I'd been here a thousand and one times before. Not here, up on this particular road and looking down over this particular ravine, I don't mean, but working on a case where I was all out of leads and found myself searching places without really knowing what I was looking for. I was feeling frustrated and bored and angry, all at the same time, if that's possible—which it must be. I kept thinking about poor old Rembrandt, and how he'd got mixed up in all this, all these years after his death.

Then I spotted something down there, lying on a shelf of rock, on the very verge of the ravine. I hunkered down to take a closer look, careful as I did so not to overbalance and take a tumble, because if I did that then it would be the last tumble I ever took. It was a book of matches. I picked it up and looked at it. The book was empty, which no doubt helped to explain what it was doing here. There was a black unicorn on the cover set against a red background. I flipped it over and saw that the name of a bar was printed on the back: BAR LOPEZ. The address was written in small print below: 297 Avenido Diego Farol, Figarillo.

Neither the name of the bar nor the address meant anything to me. I don't know Figarillo very well. I'd spent a weekend there once, and could remember a few street names and certain images but that was all. How much can anyone ever hope to see in a single weekend, anyway? And it had been a few years ago that I'd gone there.

I dropped the empty book of matches into the plastic bag, then tied the end and put it in my jacket pocket. Then I straightened up, and went back to walking up and down the roadside, on the prowl for anything that might have been discarded there. Any innocent little articles, which might or might not turn out to be every bit as innocent and innocuous as they looked.

But there were none, so I headed back down the slope and round the corner to where I'd left my car.

41

Before heading back to Bardino, I figured it might be an idea to check out the village of Magro a little.

I parked on the main street and climbed out and took a wander, until I came to a bar and went inside. It was a dark cavern of a place, so that I had a job to see anything upon first entering and had reached the tin-covered bar by the time my eyes had adjusted. The bar was empty save for a group of three old boys at the other end of the counter. It was hardly the sort of place you'd associate with a Rembrandt. Not even a stolen one.

The barman—a man in his fifties, standing at around 165 and with short black hair, a ruddy complexion and a round belly—came over and asked what he could get me. I said I'd have a Cruzcampo. When it came it was nice and cold, so that there were beads of moisture on the side of the bottle. I took a swig. It was just what the doctor ordered.

'Nice *pueblo* you've got here,' I said to the barman.

He smiled. 'Yes, I like it well enough.'

'It always this quiet?'

'Pretty much…not a lot happens here.'

I took another sip of my beer.

'You come to live here or just visiting?'

'Just passing through,' I said. 'A friend of mine has a place here.'

'Oh?'

'Inge Schwartz,' I said.

'I know her.' The man nodded. 'Pretty girl.'

'Yes, *muy guapa*.'

'I haven't seen her here for a long time,' the man said. 'Is she still living with Jaime?'

Jaime? Who was he? I wondered.

'I'm not sure if they were married or not.' The man squinted as though he were making an effort to remember. 'The house they used to stay in when they were here belongs to Jaime's cousin. They would come for a week or two and then you wouldn't see them for a while.'

I had another swig of my *cerveza*.

'They used to like to go skiing in the Sierra Nevada, I seem to recall.' The man gave me a curious up-from-under look. 'So what brings you to these parts, then?' he asked. 'Not come in the hope of finding Inge here, have you?'

'As a matter of fact,' I said, 'I was here yesterday and something unusual happened to me.' I studied the man's face closely, to see how he reacted. Whether he looked surprised or like he knew what I was about to say. But his expression didn't appear to change at all. Either he had no idea who I was or why I was here, or he was the greatest loss to the cinema or the Secret Intelligence services since Mata Hari lit out. 'I was driving along the road out of the village, you know.' There was only the one passable road, and you had to drive up the mountain a little way and back on yourself before it curled round and began to slope down. 'Anyway, I was just approaching the corner up there when a number of rocks came bounding down from the cliff face into my path. I jerked the steering wheel hard to the left, which was all I could do, and that's the last thing I recall... Perhaps you heard about it?'

'Yes, I heard something about it.' His ruddy face creased in a jovial drinker's grin. 'Still, you managed to survive it all right, I see.'

I nodded slowly, still observing him closely. 'Guess I got lucky,' I said.

'I should say you did... could've went the other way'n gone flying down the ravine.' He smiled. 'You'd done that'n you'd have been a goner.'

'Yes.' I carried on watching him, trying to make up my mind whether or not his comments were meant in all innocence. 'So what did you hear about it, then?'

'Just that someone'd crashed up there, like you said.'

'Nothing more?'

'I heard that nobody was seriously hurt.'

'What else?'

'Nothing else.'

'You sure about that?'

The jovial smile left the man's face as fast as a drunkard being expelled from a pub at closing time, and a confused sort of frown took its place. 'Not sure I follow your meaning,' he said.

'I just wondered if you heard anything else about it?'

'No... well I already told you I didn't.' He flashed me his suspicious up-from-under look again. 'Why, what was it that happened that I didn't get to hear about, then?'

'I crashed into a stone boulder on the roadside up there,' I said, 'and lost consciousness. Then when I came round, sometime later, I found that I'd been robbed.'

'No.'

'*Si*,' I said.

'What did they take? Nothing valuable, I hope?'

'A painting.'

'Oh, that's not so bad, then… I thought for a moment you was gonna say they took your bank cards, or something like that.'

'No, they left my wallet intact.'

'You were lucky in more ways than one, then,' the man said.

'Not really.'

'How come?'

'The painting was worth an awful lot of money.'

'Oh, is that so?' His eyes lit up. 'Not by some famous artist, was it?'

'It was a Rembrandt.'

He whistled softly. 'Even I've heard of him.'

I noticed a number of photographs on the wall near to where I was standing, and I turned to take a look at them. 'These photos of the villagers, are they, I take it?'

'That's right… everyone who lives in the village should be in at least one of them somewhere.'

'What about Inge?'

'Yes, she should be in there, if you look.'

I ran my eyes over the rows of smiling faces, hopping from one photograph to another, until I spotted her. She stood out like some gorgeous butterfly caught up in a crowd of moths. 'The blond chap standing next to her would be Jaime, I suppose?' I said.

The man came out from behind the bar, putting his glasses on and slipping the temple arms over his ears as he looked at the photographs.

I went up close to the photograph and pointed.

'Oh, yes, that's him.'

I brought out my iPhone and took a couple of photographs of the figure in the photograph. Then I blew them up and took a good look at the face. He was the sort of handsome bastard you'd expect to have a girl like Inge on his arm if anyone was going to. Needless to say I hated him at first sight. Arrogance and confidence seemed to stream from his very pores, the way sweat runs off a pig. His blond hair was cut short at the sides and swept across in one of those kiss curls that I'd always found desperately cheesy, but which I imagine girls must love. He was tall and slim and dressed in jeans and a navy-blue Lacoste T-shirt. His mouth was slightly parted in a surly grin, revealing white teeth. Here was a man, I thought, who'd never been made to struggle for anything. A man for whom doors would have been opened before he even bothered to knock on them. Well, I for one should have liked to slam a few in his face. I turned my head to look at the barman and said, 'Do you know if anyone in the village comes from Figarillo, or if any of the villagers have been up there recently?'

He shrugged. 'Can't say I do,' he said. 'Although now that you mention it, Inge herself was from Figarillo originally, I think.'

I left a couple of coins on the counter. 'Nice talking to you,' I said, and then I turned and made for the door.

'Any time,' the man called after me.

42

I went back to my car and wondered what my next move ought to be. As I was wondering, I began to ponder upon the book of matches I'd found up on the road. I'd just started the engine up and set off, when somebody popped up from the floor under the back seat. Whoever it was held a gun to the back of my head. 'Long time no see,' he said.

Moving my eyes only, I looked in the mirror to see who it was. And recognized the big man in the suit who worked for Vince Caportorio. 'What are you doing here?'

'My boss wants to see you.'

'I don't want to see him.'

'That's not very nice.'

'He's not a very nice guy.'

'He likes you a lot.'

'Does he always try to kill the people he likes?'

'He didn't try to kill you,' the fat guy said. 'I did.' I could see him grinning at me in the mirror. 'Now I want you to reach into your pocket real slow and take your gun out. Any fast movements and I'll shoot, understand?'

'Shoot me and I'll crash.'

'I'll take my chances on that,' he said. 'I want you to hold the gun by the barrel and hand it back to me, okay?'

I did as I'd been told. Then I said, 'So how come you didn't kill me that time, huh?'

'Never mind, Arthur, you know what they say about if at first you don't succeed and all that jazz.'

'Can't you come up with anything more original than that?' I said. 'That line must been six centuries old.'

'The old ones are always the best, don't you know that?'

'Do you apply that rule to everything in life?'

'Pretty much.'

'You mean you like your women old, too?'

'That supposed to be funny, Arthur?'

'I dunno, you tell me.'

'I don't think it's funny, but I think you do,' he said. 'Think you're cute, don't you?'

'If you say so.'

'Why don't you shut the fuck up and drive.'

'That's what I was just about to do,' I said.

'Yeah, only we ain't going where you was about to go.'

'So where are we going?'

'I already told you–Vince wantsa see you.'

'So where's that?'

'Just keep driving and I'll tell you where.'

The sun was turning the screw by now and my shirt was as wet as a rainy Sunday in Shrewsbury, which is pretty damn wet. I drove up to the next corner and, as I rounded it, so memories of my last date with Vince flitted through my mind. How could I ever forget it? Vince's hospitality was certainly of the sort that leaves an indelible mark on the memory. Most hosts don't dip you in the family pool by way of introducing you to their pet shark, after all. I guess dinner parties would go out of fashion pretty quickly if they did. I never did get to rub cheeks with the toothy Estrella, but it had been a close call. Now if there was ever a girl to whom the term 'man eater' truly applied then it was her. To rub cheeks with her was to lose your head, literally.

It's funny the way a man can get to thinking when he's scared. I figured my time was up unless I could shake off the bruiser on the back seat; but I didn't see how I might do that, given that he had a gun pointed at my head.

I drove in silence for quite some time, and then the coastline came into view. 'I know I'm a nice and friendly kinda guy,' I said, 'but I really don't see why someone like Vince should go to such lengths to seek out my company.'

'Vince wants to see a guy, he sees him.'

'But what's it all about? I mean I never did get to find out during my first visit.'

'You could try asking him, see what he says.'

'Maybe I will,' I said.

When I turned the next corner, I found my path blocked by a large black van. 'Stop here and get out.'

I considered my options for a fraction of a second, until I felt the muzzle of the mutt's gun against the back of my skull and figured I'd better do as he said. When we got out of the car, the back of the van opened. And there was Vince grinning at me. 'Get in,' he said.

Vince Caportorio looked at me. I couldn't see his eyes because he was wearing shades, but I figured I wasn't missing much. 'Where's the Rembrandt?' he said.

'I thought you had it.'

'Still trying to bullshit me, huh?' He shook his head. 'Listen, you haven't told me what you did with it by the time we get home, I'm going to let Estrella have you this time. Poor thing hasn't eaten for a coupla days. Starved her just for you.'

'Very thoughtful of you.'

'She'll appreciate you all the more.'

'Look,' I said, 'I'm telling you the truth.'

43

Vince took off his shades, blew on the lenses, then took out a rag and began to wipe them. 'You ain't so stupid that you don't know you're gonna talk one way or the other,' he said. 'So you may as well make it easy on yourself.'

'Okay,' I said, 'I'll tell you everything.'

'Make it short and sweet,'cause patience ain't my strong point.'

'She sent me up to her house in Magro, to retrieve the Rembrandt. She had it stashed away there in a secret place.'

'Why'd she want to send you to pick it up?' Vince was looking at me now, a frown on his face like I'd got his interest.

'I was working for her... I thought you knew. Her sister Gisela'd been kidnapped—by you, I assume—and she wanted me to go and get the Rembrandt.'

'You might've run off with it.'

'I might've done if I was a crook, but I'm not.'

I saw the corners of Vince's mouth turn up, like he found the idea of my not running off with the Rembrandt, or even wanting to, vaguely amusing.

'Anyway, I'm sure you know the rest.'

'Tell me anyway.'

'I was ambushed by you or your mutts after I left the village.'

'Ambushed?' He seemed surprised. 'News to me.'

'You mean it was you that did it?'

He shook his head. 'Tell me about it.'

'Coming down the mountain,' I said. 'Some rocks came tumbling down into my path and nearly killed me. I swerved to avoid them and crashed into a rock jutting out of the cliff face at the side of the road. I lost consciousness and when I came round the Rembrandt was gone.'

'So who took it?'

'No idea,' I said. 'I mean, I figured it must be you or the guys you've got working for you.'

'What made you jump to that conclusion?'

'I remembered from the time I was at your house that you seemed to be very keen to get your hands on the painting.'

'I was,' he said, 'and still am.'

'You mean it really wasn't you that took it?'

'No.'

'Was it you that kidnapped Gisela?'

'Think I'll take the Fifth on that one.'

'So why did you kill her?'

'I didn't.' He grinned. 'You did.'

'Very funny... but why kill her and then dump the body in my living room?'

'Don't ask me, I dunno the way these criminals operate.' He stifled a theatrical yawn. 'Suppose you can follow the logic, though, can't you?'

'What logic?'

'Imagine you was the kidnapper,' he said. 'You set a deadline. The person you've taken's gonna get it if the ransom ain't delivered by whenever it is...then the person you're dealing with fails to deliver, so the sister that's been kidnapped has to go.'

'Okay, but why dump the body on my sofa?'

'Frame you, old chap, I suppose.' He chuckled. 'Thought you might turn out to be of some use to me, even if you weren't to your client.'

'What about Juan Ribera and Joaquim Gross?'

'The fuck're they?'

'The two gangsters that got it in the neck.'

'If I was a bettin' man,'Vince said, 'then judging from what you just told me, I shouldn't be surprised if they was a coupla wannabes trying to poke their nose in where it wasn't wanted. Rembrandt's a very popular artist, so I've heard.'

'And it sounds as though he's every bit as much of a hit with the criminal underground as he is with the art lovers and critics.'

'I shouldn't doubt it, seeing how much money's on the end of it.'

I ran a hand over my face as I considered what I'd just learned. 'So who took the Rembrandt, then?'

'That's the question. Not to be or not to fucking be, but where's the fuckin' Rembrandt?'

'There must've been someone else who knew about it.'

'Unless you're feeding me porkies.'

Vince Caportorio was close enough for me to be able to smell his sweat and stink, and the thought that the man was going to get away scot-free made me sick. Then I remembered Javier Fontana and said, 'Did you kill the hack that got dead on my sofa, too, Vince?'

'If I were you, Arthur, I'd do something about that sofa of yours.'

'Yeah? What would you do about it?'

'I'd start by throwing it out.'

'How come?'

'Just hearing you say about those two young people that got dead on it,' he said. 'You ask me, that don't sound too good.'

'It wasn't the sofa that killed them.'

'I dunno.'

'What don't you know about, Vince?'

'I wouldn't have a sofa like that in my home, that's for sure.'

'You got a shark there.'

'She's different.'

'She's *that* all right.'

'Sofa like that sounds to me like it got the voodoo or something.'

'Have you got African blood, Vince?'

'No, I ain't.'

'But I thought voodoo's what the Africans believe in, isn't it?'

'What the fuck,' he said. 'All's I'm sayin's that I would get that sofa checked out. Or better still, I'd throw it out.' He appeared to consider what he'd just said and shrugged. 'Little late now, though, I suppose, seeing as where you're going.'

I looked at Vince and he looked at me. I thought he was a no-good ugly bastard, and from the expression on his mug it was safe to assume he felt similar sentiments where I was concerned. 'What with all this talk about my sofa,' I said, 'you still haven't answered my question.'

'Question's that?'

'Why you killed the hack.'

'Hacks can be a nuisance, I find.'

'Hacks in general, do you mean? Or are you talking about the one particular hack?'

Vince shrugged. 'The fuck makes you so curious?'

'It's my job, remember?'

'You're gonna die anyway.'

'We're all headed that way, Vince. Haven't you heard?'

'Yeah, but you're gonna head there a lot sooner'n most.'

I didn't like the sound of that, but I tried not to let it show. 'His name was Javier Fontana.'

'Who was?'

'The hack.'

'You still talking about him?'

'Came all the way down from Figarillo.'

'Nice for him.'

'Not so nice, I should've said, all things considered.'

'Already told you, hacks are a nuisance. They're like flies on a joint of meat. Who needs them?'

Just then, we slowed down, and moments later the van came to a halt. The driver got out and came and opened the doors at the back, and the mutt with the peashooter told me to get out first. I did as I was told, and any thoughts I might have had of making a move were cancelled out when I saw the gun that the guy who'd been driving was pointing at me. It was a Walther PKK. A small piece, but the punch it packed if you got it angry was more than big enough to put a hole in a man.

The mutt poked me in the back with his pen and I moved like a line of prose. A shaky line of prose that was sweating and shaking with fear. 'We're going into the house,' he said.

If ever there was a reluctant guest, then I was that man as I trudged forward towards the large white farmhouse. I just kept telling myself that I had to make my move, but there was no way I could do so with the mutt there behind me, jabbing his pen in my back.

The house was quite a place, but I was in no mood to appreciate the superior architecture and swanky interior. All I could think about was how many people had died under the man's roof, and whether I was going to be an addition to that number. I found myself being shoved through the house and out back to where the pool was. By now my guts were turning over. It's one thing to get killed, but to end up being eaten alive by a hungry shark is something else. And what made it worse was knowing that it was going to happen in advance. No words can express it, so I won't even bother to go there. I tried to make a run for it, but I'd left it too late and there was nowhere for me to go. Vince had his mutts hold me down, and then they trussed me up like the Christmas turkey, the way they had on my previous visit, and the next thing I know I'm being hoisted out over the pool. They lower me down and my nose is full of the smell of the chlorine in the water, and I can hear Vince chuckling away to himself like he finds all of this just so fucking amusing.

Looking below, I could see the shark circling. She was a big beast and I just hoped that it would be over quickly. It hurt like hell to think that Vince was going to get away with all this. Then I got to thinking what a lot of stupid oafs the local cops were, to have allowed Vince to get away with so much killing for so long. And to think he was here living in this palace he had for a home, like some latter day king. All this flashed through my mind as I watched the shark circling beneath the water.

Then I felt myself being lowered until my head was just a couple of inches from the surface of the water. Out of the corner of my eye I could see the shark's fin moving up the other end of the pool, some thirty metres or so away. I saw the beast turn as it got to the far end, and then start to make its way back towards me. It wouldn't take her long now, only a matter of seconds...

Just then, I heard someone shouting, then a gunshot rang out. The fin was cutting through the surface of the water like an electronic saw through butter. The creature moved with an oily sleekness. It was an efficient underwater killer. A beast that seemed to my mind to do little other than kill and eat, and then procreate. I'd never had much time for sharks. To my way of thinking they're mean, cold-hearted killers, just like Vince. And what I was going through now wasn't likely to change my mind on that score.

44

I heard more gunfire. Something was going on in the house, although quite what it was I couldn't begin to imagine. I heard Vince barking at his mutts. At least he wasn't laughing anymore. But what was going on? I wondered, as the shark passed right underneath me, and I watched it go on up to the other end of the pool. It was checking me out, I thought. Now it knew I was here, so next time it would probably make its move.

I heard more gunfire, then something or somebody fell into the pool with a splash. Craning my neck, I saw the shark's fin as the beast glided through the water. Then I heard screams, and saw the shark's head come up out of the water. It had a man's legs in its mouth. The water was red with blood. Somebody had clearly come a cropper. I wondered who. And what was all the shouting and gunfire about?

I saw the shark's fin moving through the water towards me once more. It was some fifteen metres away from me now, and I knew that I was soon going to end up like the guy who'd just been chewed in half. Then just as the shark was about to get me, I felt myself being hoisted up through the air. What was going on? I wondered.

Moments later, I was lowered onto the tiles at the side of the pool, and three men were untying me. I recognized one of them. It was Inspector Jefe Salvador Cobos. 'Sal,' I said, 'it's you of all people.'

'None other.' He grinned. 'Seems like you had a lucky escape, Arthur.'

I was giddy when they stood me up, so that they had to hold me to prevent me from falling. All that hanging upside hadn't done much to improve my directional sense, and I wouldn't have known which way was north from a bunch of bananas. But Sal had his men help me through the house out to one of the squad cars parked out front. A policewoman came over and offered me a cup of coffee. I took it and drank. It tasted like sawdust. But even drinking bad coffee beats getting eaten by a shark, so I wasn't about to complain.

'You look kinda the worse for wear,' the officer said.

'I always get like this after I've had a workout,' I told her.

She nodded like she knew what I meant, but then she gave me this sly look like she couldn't quite make me out.

Within the hour Sal Cobos and I were talking over a drink in Marco's, a little place off the seafront in Bardino. Sal seemed to have his nice hat on. He'd just bought me a large Scotch, anyway. We were sitting at the wooden counter, and the television was on up on the wall. Some film with Al Pacino. The barmaid was busy washing glasses.

Sal grinned and said, 'Seems like it's your lucky day, Arthur.'

'I guess.'

'We hadn't arrived I dread to think what would've happened to you.' He sipped his Ballantines. 'You'd've ended up like that other guy, worked for Vince. Shark severed his legs from his trunk.'

'How did that happen?'

'He fell into the pool in the fighting that took place, after we arrived on the scene.'

'Fell or was pushed?'

'His own stupid fault.' Sal shrugged. 'Some of my officers are tough, but none of them would've wanted to see what happened to that man happen to anyone.'

Something occurred to me. 'I thought you said Vince was planning on having a quiet night in with his ladylove?'

Sal grinned. 'Guess he must've changed his mind.'

I nodded and took a sip of my Scotch, figuring there really wasn't much to be said about the matter. I'd nearly been killed, but I got lucky. That was it. Sal didn't seem to feel quite the same way about it, though. 'You must feel pretty shook up about it still, I should think,' he said. 'Nearly getting eaten alive like you did.'

I shrugged. 'It's over now.'

'So it hasn't made you have second thoughts about what you do for a living?'

'Are you kidding me?'

'No, I'm being serious, Arthur. You've just been through a harrowing experience that would affect any man.'

'It was harrowing when it happened,' I told him. 'But it's not harrowing anymore.'

'How come?'

'I didn't get eaten, did I?'

Sal laughed. 'Simple as that, huh?'

'Simple as that.'

He laughed again. I couldn't see the joke. 'You must have some balls,' he said, 'that's all I can say.'

'Not really. I was scared while it happened. But that was then, and now is now. It's over and I'm okay.'

He nodded thoughtfully. 'So what was it all about, Arthur?'

'You tell me, Sal.'

'I was hoping you might be a little more forthcoming,' he said. 'After all, we did come and rescue you.'

'That's true... how did you know I'd be there, anyway?'

'We followed you.' Sal took a Camel from the pack on the wooden counter, put it between his lips and lit it. 'I knew you'd be getting up to something.' He squinted, rubbed at his eyes as grey ribbons of smoke billowed from him. 'You're a mysterious man, Arthur. I mean just take the way people seem to've developed the nasty habit of getting dead around you.' He smiled. 'So we wanted to keep tabs on you and see what you were getting up to... And we still want to find out.'

I figured I owed Sal something, all things considered. 'Okay,' I said. 'I was ambushed coming out of Magro yesterday. When I came round, a certain article I'd gone to pick up for my client had gone.'

'Care to shed a little more light on the nature of the article that went missing?'

'It was a Rembrandt original.'

Sal Cobos made an O with his lips and whistled. 'So somebody was expecting you, you're saying?'

'Must've been.'

Sal nodded, took a drag on his Camel. 'Wait a minute,' he said, 'this all happened up in Magro, you say?'

'That's right.'

'You mean that Inge Schwartz had a Rembrandt original stashed away there?'

'In a house in the village.'

'So what's happened to it?'

'Wish I knew.' I shrugged.

'Mm.' Sal Cobos tasted his Scotch. 'So where does Vince Cap come into all this?'

'I went back to Magro, like I said, to try and work out what happened when I was robbed, and see if I could perhaps remember anything or talk to somebody who saw something.'

'Did you?'

'I talked to the man who runs the bar in the village.'

'He see anything?'

'No.'

'So then what?'

'I'm driving home and one of Vince's mutts pops up from below the back seat.'

'Takes you to see Vince and he wants to know where the Rembrandt is or he's gonna feed you to his shark.'

'That's it.'

'I know because we were watching you from further up the mountain, and we tailed you once you got into the van.' Cobos gave his nose a thoughtful scratch. 'So Inge Schwartz has asked you to retrieve her Rembrandt for her?'

'Correct.'

Sal looked at me. 'Any idea where it is?'

'Nope.' I sipped my Scotch. 'That's why I went back to Magro, but I was just clutching at straws.'

'So now what are you going to do?'

'Keep looking, I guess.'

'But where?'

'Where'd somebody go if they had a Rembrandt to sell?'

'Good question, Arthur.' He ground what was left of his cigarette to death in the ashtray. 'Can't imagine it would be easy to sell one around these parts.'

'Unless it was stolen to order.'

'I doubt that very much. People I've spoken to who know about these things tell me that rumours of that sort of thing happening are all just that–rumours. I mean just think about it, Arthur. Imagine you're some rich guy. Would you really want to shell out a few million to men you probably can't trust for what amounts to stolen property?'

'Maybe you're right,' I said. 'But they must think they're going to sell it somewhere.'

'Could just've been an opportunist. Somebody who gets to hear that you've gone to Magro for the Rembrandt and spots his chance.'

'But I didn't tell anybody why I was going there.'

'So what do you reckon, then—any ideas?'

'No, not really.' I finished my drink, then slid off my stool. 'Better be off now, Sal,' I said. 'Been nice to catch up, and thanks for the Scotch.'

'Stay and have another one.'

'I need to go and pick up my car.' I smiled. 'Wouldn't want me to be driving under the influence, now would you?'

As I reached the door, Sal Cobos called to me and I turned. 'What?'

'Take my advice and stay clear of water for a while.'

45

When I got home I checked the place out before entering, just to make sure nobody was about to spring out on me, because I'd had enough surprises for one day. The place was empty, though, and everything was cool. There were no bodies on the sofa, dead or otherwise–or anywhere else in the flat for that matter.

I was feeling tired, so I took a long hot bath and then I went to bed and slept right through till the middle of the following morning. I'm normally one of these types who find it hard to drop off, but it's surprising what having been scared out of your wits will do for your capacity to sleep. Not that it was a particularly peaceful night for me, because I had a nightmare about being in a swimming pool with a shark.

After I'd showered, I logged onto my laptop and booked myself onto the next flight to Figarillo. It had just turned 2 p.m. when the plane touched down. I hurried through Passport Controls and passed out through the electronic doors, then took a taxi into the centre of the town, where I booked myself into a room in a shabby two star hotel. Then I went out and found an Avis outlet, where I rented a Lexus, and I took a drive over to Calle Diego Farol and pulled up outside of a place called Bar López. There were a few people sitting at plastic tables on the pavement, enjoying the sunshine. I sat there for a long time, watching the front of the bar, and nothing much seemed to be going on. Then I started to get the feeling I was being watched. I wasn't totally sure, but the guy sitting in the Seat Ibiza that was parked across the street had sure been there a long time.

I figured it might be an idea to run a little test, just to see if the man was watching me. So I started the engine up and set off. And sure enough, the guy tailed me. He was trying not to make it too obvious, because there were two cars between mine and his, but he was there in my mirror all right. Now as a man who spends a fair amount of his time searching for and watching and following others, it rather sticks in my craw when people think they can tail *me.* I suppose that's just human nature for you. Anyway, I decided to have a little fun with the guy. So I took a left, then started zigzagging my way through the streets, and sure enough the Seat Ibiza came after me.

I pulled over outside of a hotel and, seeing my shadow pull over some forty metres behind me, I climbed out of my Porsche and crossed the road, locking the doors with the remote without looking back. I entered the hotel–the Don Carlos, I think it was called. It was a big and fairly classy place–the sort of establishment you wouldn't normally find me dead in on account of the prices they charge; but this was different. I crossed the lobby. There had to be a back way out of a place this big, I thought. It was just a case of finding it, which I did easily enough. Then having left the hotel, I went up to the corner and found myself looking across at my shadow. He was sitting behind the wheel of his Seat Ibiza, watching the entrance I'd gone in through like a jealous husband spying on his wife. I took out my shades and put them on, then set off across the road. I walked quickly, and was at the man's side before he'd noticed my approach.

'*Buenas tardes*,' I said in his ear, and the guy almost jumped out of his seat.

46

His brown eyes were flashing alarm signals as he turned to look at me. '*Buenas tardes.*'

I looked at him closely as I tried to work out whether I knew his face from somewhere. Late twenties, maybe early thirties, on the skinny side, thinning brown hair, brown eyes–his face sure didn't ring any bells with me. So why was the guy following me? Perhaps he was a fellow private eye, or else a plainclothes cop, who'd been hired to tail me. But somehow he just didn't look the type. Too pale and nervous.

'Sorry,' he said, 'but I don't think we've met.'

'No, I don't believe we have.' I grinned at him. 'But it looks to me like you're pretty keen to change that.'

His mouth opened, but no words came out.

'Who are you and why have you been tailing me?'

'Sorry,' he said, seeming to relax a little now that he realized he'd been rumbled. 'I'm a reporter.'

I brought out my gun and pointed it at his temple. 'Got some ID you can show me?'

'Sure, but there's no need for the gun.'

'I'll be the judge of that,' I said. 'And it had better be your ID you bring out of your jacket or your brains are gonna make a mess of your nice new upholstery.'

'I'm not carrying a weapon.'

'Easy does it.'

'Okay.' He reached inside his jacket and brought out his wallet. 'Here.'

'You open it for me.'

'Sure.'

He held it out so that I could see it. I read from the man's card that his name was Miguel Pasqual and that he was a staff reporter for *La Vanguardia*.

'Okay,' I said, 'you can put it away and move over.'

'What?'

'Onto the passenger seat. It's time you and I had a little talk.'

He did as he was told, and I put my gun away, then opened the door and climbed in behind the wheel. 'I won't bother to waste time introducing myself,' I said, 'because you obviously know already who I am. But I think you owe me an explanation.'

'Javier Fontana, the reporter who was killed, was a colleague and a good friend of mine,' he said. 'He was investigating a story that took him down to Bardino, and somehow he ended up dead in your flat.'

'On my sofa, to be precise.'

'Which is why I've been following you.'

'You thought I had something to do with your friend's death?

'Did you?'

'No, I'm a private detective.'

'That doesn't tell me much.'

'Somebody was trying to frame me for his and other murders.'

'I understand that you're working for Inge Schwartz?'

'Who told you that?' I asked. 'And how did you know I was in Figarillo?'

'I didn't,' he replied. 'I came here for the same reason you did.'

'What makes you think you know why I'm here?'

'I noticed you were keeping an eye on the same things I am, so I got curious about you.' He shrugged. 'I called a friend and gave him your reg number and asked him to check you out.'

'But hacks don't normally tail guys like me around.'

'They do if they want a story badly enough.'

I figured the guy was probably on the level.

'Look,' Pasqual said, 'I've got some information about your client that might be of use to you, but I can't see why I should level with you if you don't want to play straight with me.'

'What information's this?'

'So she is your client,' he said.

I looked at Pasqual and he looked right back at me. He might have had a scrawny build, but he had a determined, ballsy look about him. I said, 'Why do you ask me questions you already know the answer to?'

'Do you trust her?'

'Why do you ask that?'

'Just answer yes or no.'

'I wouldn't be working for her if I didn't.'

Pasqual chuckled and I asked him what was so funny. 'I guess she must've got under your skin, huh?' he said.

'Hardly surprising, because she sure is a babe...the sort can wrap any man round her garter string whenever she feels like it.'

'Don't sound as if you like her very much.'

'I don't know her personally.'

'So why're you so keen to give her a bad press?'

'I'm out to get at the truth,' he said. 'That's the bottom line for me.'

'Sounds like we're both travelling on the same train.'

He looked at me like he was trying to read me. 'How much do you know about her?'

I shrugged. 'She employed me to find her sister.'

'And she ended up dead on your hands, too, right?'

I nodded and blew out my cheeks as I remembered the sight of Gisela Schwartz's body lying there on my sofa. Her eyes staring up at me as I went in and looked at her. The feeling of shock I experienced. 'I found her all right,' I said. 'Only it was too late.'

'So who killed her?'

'Guy who kidnapped her.'

'And who was that?'

I looked at him. 'You're doing a pretty good job of milking me, kid,' I said. 'What about a little *quid pro quo* here?'

'What do you want to know?'

'You were going to let me in on some information you had on my client.'

'Sure,' he said. 'Her father, you know about him?'

'No. Should I?'

'It might interest you to know that he was a rich art dealer,' Miguel Pasqual said. He reached into the pocket of the leather jacket he was wearing, brought out a pack of Marlboros. 'Want one?'

'No, thanks.'

'Been trying to give up, but haven't got very far with it.' He took out a cigarette and lodged it between his lips, then brought out a Zippo and lit it. I watched him take a long drag.

'Look like you needed that.'

'I did,' he said.

'Only one way to do it,' I said, 'and that's to make a clean break.'

'You talk like it's easy.'

'Talking about it is easy. It's doing it that's the tough part.'

'Like anything, I guess... difference between talking the talk and walking the walk.'

'You got it.'

I sat in silence for a moment and watched him smoke. 'Your client spent some time at school in Germany as a kid, so she speaks the lingo and can pass herself off as a Kraut easily enough. But she's actually from Figarillo, and her real name's Barbara Borrell. Her father made his money back in the days of the regime,' he resumed. 'Sold stuff on the black market. You name it, he could get it for you's what they used to say about him, so I understand. He becomes friendly with General Franco, which doesn't do his business interests any harm whatsoever–quite the reverse in fact, as I'm sure you'll understand. Rumour is he'd get basic foodstuffs on the cheap by using his connections, back in the days when Franco was doing his best to screw up the economy, and then he'd sell whatever it was for several times what he paid out. It was the next best thing to having a license to print money for a guy like him, lacking in scruples as he was. Cut a story short, it's not long before he's stinking rich. But he's keen to get respectable, so he invests his money in art treasures. I guess he probably figured that being an art collector had a certain ring to it, a certain cachet that might perfume over the stink of where his millions actually came from. Whatever. Fast forward a few decades and he leaves his entire art collection to a state museum.'

'What about his daughters?'

'Didn't leave them a single penny—or painting.'

'Bet they were happy about that.'

'Deliriously so, I'm sure.' Pasqual took a last drag on his cigarette before he crash-landed it into the ashtray. 'The girls contested it, of course, and the collection was frozen as a result.'

'Because of the court case?'

'Exactly. The art works were all held at the family mansion, which was locked up, and the understanding was that they were to be kept there until the case had been concluded. But then, surprise, surprise, a few of the paintings, among them the pick of the bunch as it turns out, go walkies and nobody seems to have any idea where they are. The most famous work in the entire collection is a certain Rembrandt. It's a small work, but of great value and it's gone missing.'

'Sounds like it must be the one that the kidnapper was asking for as ransom,' I said.

'Did she hand it over to him?'

'No. She asked me to do it, but I was ambushed on the way.'

'So now she's asked you to get it back?'

'That's right.'

'What made you come here of all places?'

I told him about the book of matches I'd found and where I'd come by it. 'I put two and two together,' I said. 'Javier Fontana was killed after he came from this city to investigate a story that involved my client.'

'So you reckoned all roads must lead to Figarillo, and to this café in particular?'

'You tell me,' I said. 'What exactly was it that brought you here?'

'Place has got a rep in certain quarters as being the place to come if you want to make contacts in the art world,' he replied. 'Rumour has it you can buy all manner of stuff in there that's not on the menu, if you get my meaning.'

'Call in for a cappuccino and find yourself being talked into buying a stolen Canaletto?'

'Exactly. Or order a panini and the waiter thinks you're using the word as a proper noun and gives you a list of titles with the corresponding dimensions.'

'I never knew there was a painter called Panini.'

'You learn something every day.' Pasqual grinned. 'Best known perhaps for his view of the interior of the Pantheon.'

'Sounds like an interesting menu they do over there,' I said. 'I wonder if a certain stolen Rembrandt might not be the order of the day.'

'I can see our thoughts are starting to converge.'

'I think it's high time I took a little wander over there.'

'Worked up an appetite, have you?'

'Sitting around here watching people eat's hungry work.'

'You bet it is,' Pasqual said. 'I'll stay here a while, and perhaps you'd like to keep me updated on how you get on. I mean, we could work as a team on this.'

'Okay, so long as you don't print anything until I've got to the bottom of it. If you do, our marriage is over.'

'Wouldn't dream of it.'

'Wish me luck,' I said, and climbed out of the car.

47

It was a long rectangular-shaped joint, with round wooden tables big enough for two, or three at a pinch. I sat by the window and reached that day's *El Pais* down from the rack that was on the wall just behind me. Not that I was in a mood to read the news, but it gave me something to do, as well as something to hide behind if it became necessary for me to do so.

I heard the waiter's shoes clunking over the polished wooden boards as he approached my table. He said '*Buenos dias*', a skinny guy in a white shirt and bow tie. I bade him good morning in return, and he handed me a card menu and asked if I was ready to order. I said I'd have a croissant and coffee. The man said,'*Muy bien*,'then turned and went off. When he returned with my order, minutes later, he smiled and asked me if I was here on holiday. 'That's right,' I told him. 'Just taking a few days out.'

He scratched at his handlebar tash and said, 'Figarillo's a beautiful city and there's plenty to see and do here.'

'So I gather.' I smiled. 'I'm particularly interested in checking out the city's galleries.'

'You take an interest in art, *señor*?'

'Sure do.'

'Who is your favourite artist?'

'There are so many,' I said.

'But if you had to pick one?'

'It would have to be Rembrandt.' I watched him closely as I said this, but didn't observe any noticeable change in his expression or manner. I decided to push the matter to its natural conclusion and see where it took me. 'Fact of the matter is,' I said, 'I've heard there's one on sale over here and I'm interested in making an offer.'

'A Rembrandt, *señor*?'

'Yes.'

'For sale?'

'So I've heard.'

'How interesting,' he said. 'Where did you come by this information?'

'I have friends who take an interest in the international art market, and they keep me updated on what's going on.'

'How fortunate for you.'

'I guess so.' I smiled. 'Don't tell me that you're an art lover, too?'

'I certainly am.'

'In that case, I don't suppose you'd be able to help me?'

'Help you, *señor*?'

'Find out about this Rembrandt that's for sale?'

'Which Rembrandt would this be?'

I told him the name of the work.

'I can certainly keep an ear out for you, *señor*.'

'I'd be very grateful if you would,' I said. 'And there'd be some money in it for you, of course.'

The man ditched his false smile and Vaseline charm. 'If you come back here tomorrow around the same time, I'll see if I can manage to turn something up for you.'

'I appreciate it.' I took out a fifty-euro note. 'Keep the change,' I said, 'as a little token of gratitude.'

'*Gracias.*'

It didn't take me long to make my breakfast of *café con leche* and croissant disappear, then I got up and went out. The hack, Miguel Pasqual, was still waiting in his car across the street.

I went over and climbed in beside him.

'How did it go?'

'Just put out some feelers,' I said. 'Man told me to come back tomorrow, same time same place, and he might have something for me.'

'That sounds promising.'

'Maybe, maybe not.' I smiled. 'Just thought I'd tell you now, so you'll know where to come and won't need to keep following me everywhere I go until then.'

'I appreciate it.' He killed his cigarette. 'I get the feeling this could be the start of a beautiful friendship.'

'If you don't want it all to end it tears, just make sure you keep your promise and don't print anything until it's all over.'

'I already gave you my word.'

'That's right, you did.' I climbed back out of the car, then leaned over and said, 'Till tomorrow,' before I slammed the door.

I figured that I ought to check my new buddy out, just to make sure he was the hack he claimed to be. So no sooner had I climbed in behind the wheel of my Porsche than I took out my iPhone, then I drove up to the car Pasqual was parked in, and as I drew level I came to a stop and called to him. 'Hey, Miguel,' I said.

He turned and looked at me. 'What?'

'Don't be late tomorrow.' I held my iPhone up as I spoke, and pushed the button to take a photograph of him. Then I drove off. The next time I had to stop for a red light, I ran a Google search to find the number for the head office of *La Vanguardia*, the newspaper. The light changed to green just as I got the number up, and I made the call with my left hand while I used my right to steer. A woman picked up and said, '*La Vanguardia,* head office,' and I asked her if a Miguel Pasqual worked for the newspaper. Then when the woman replied in the affirmative, I asked if I could speak to him. 'I'm afraid he's out of the office at the moment,' she said. 'Is there anybody else that might be able to help you?'

'Could I come in and talk to someone?'

'What's it concerning?'

'The journalist who was killed, Javier Fontana.'

'Oh...are you a policeman?'

'Yes,' I lied.

The woman asked me to wait while she got someone else to talk to me. The line went dead for a short while, then a man came on. 'Jorge Roig speaking,' he said.

I told him that I was investigating the death of Javier Fontana, and asked if I could come in and talk to him or one of his colleagues who knew anything about the story that Fontana had been working on. 'But I've already spoken to you people,' Roig said.

'Truth is, I'm a private investigator.'

'So why don't you go and ask the police what they know?'

'They can be a little cagey with private investigators,' I said. 'Seem to resent the competition.'

'Well I'm sorry to hear that, Mr. uh–'

'Blakey. Arthur Blakey.'

'Yes, I'm sorry to hear that, as I say, Mr. Blakey, but quite frankly I've already spent a lot of time talking to the cops and precious little seems to have come of it.'

'But you want to see whoever killed your colleague brought to justice, right?'

'Of course I do…we all do. But there doesn't seem to be any sign of that happening.'

'Look,' I said, 'before you hang up, perhaps I ought to tell you that it was me Javier Fontana came to see before he was killed.'

'Oh…well what did he want to see you about?'

'That's just it, you see I'm not sure,' I said. 'He was killed before I got to talk to him… Now I'm trying to find the man's killer so he can be brought to justice.'

'Who are you working for?'

'A private client.'

'Mind telling me who this client of yours is?'

'I'm afraid I can't tell you that.'

'Sounds to me like you want me to help you, and the first time I ask you a question you refuse to answer it.'

'No private investigator worth his salt would,' I told him. 'It goes with the job…same with journalists and their sources sometimes, isn't it?'

'Guess so.' He coughed down the line. 'So are you saying you actually spoke to Javier Fontana?'

'Yes,' I said. 'Look, I can tell you about this, if you'll agree to meet me.'

'Okay, if you can come over at three this afternoon,' he said. 'Ask for me at the switchboard, and I'll come down and meet you. I'll try and find out as much as I can about it by then.'

'Thanks. Until later, then.'

We hung up. It was just coming up to 2 a.m., so I drove over to the newspaper's offices and parked, then I got out and found a café. I sat at a vacant table outside, and had the waiter bring me a newspaper and a glass of *cerveza*, and I used up an hour or so poring over the news. Then I paid the bill and headed into the office building across the street, went over to the reception desk, and asked to speak to Jorge Roig.

The girl on reception called Roig, to tell him I'd come to see him, and he came down almost straightaway. A stocky man in his forties, dressed in a grey pinstripe number, he looked like he'd just crawled out from under a pile of assignments. 'I was just going to the cafe,' he said, 'so we can talk over a drink.'

'Sure.'

I followed his stocky frame out through the glass doors, and we walked up to the next corner and entered a little place just along on the left. Jorge Roig ran a hand over his mouth and black chinstrap beard and blinked his eyes a couple of times. 'So you wanted to speak to me about Javier Fontana,' he said.

'That's right.'

'I haven't been able to talk to anyone about it since you called.' He puffed out his cheeks and blinked again. 'One of those days, I'm afraid. Most days are, come to think of it.'

'Busy?'

'And some.' He scratched his nose. 'Javier was a good man and a good reporter,' he said. 'If I can help you in any way then I will.'

The waitress came over. A slim brunette in her thirties, she smiled at the journalist and asked him how he was keeping. 'Can't complain, Carmen. What about you?'

'Oh I'm not so bad.'

'Your mother okay?'

'Not so good.'

The girl began to tell Jorge Roig about her mother's ailments, and the journalist listened with apparent sympathy. 'Oh well,' he said, 'I hope she gets better.'

The waitress offered up a sad smile, full of resignation, then she asked us what she could get us. '*Café con leche* for me,' Jorge Roig said.

'And I'll have one, too.'

The waitress turned and disappeared.

'Look,' I said, 'I've just been talking to a Miguel Pasqual, who tells me he's a reporter for *La Vanguardia*.'

'That's right.'

I got the photo I'd taken of him up on my iPhone and held it out, so Roig could see it. 'Mind telling me,' I said, 'if this is him?'

'Nope, that's not him.'

'You totally sure about that?'

'Positive,' Jorge Roig said. 'I know Miguel Pasqual. He's a colleague of mine–and that's not him.'

'Thanks.'

'You sound surprised,' he said. 'But what's all this about?'

'Seems like somebody's been pretending to be your colleague, that's all.'

'But why'd they do that?'

'To trick me into trusting him, I guess.' And into leading him to the Rembrandt, I thought. Although I saw no reason why I should share everything I knew with this journalist whom I'd only just met. He'd only write it up in his newspaper. And if he did that then he'd let whoever the guy was that was pretending to be Pasqual know he'd been rumbled. That wasn't what I wanted. I preferred to let the guy think I'd bought what he told me.

Jorge Roig frowned, ran a chubby hand through his short black hair. 'Shouldn't be surprised if it was some freelance trying to rustle up a story,' he said. 'We've had that in the past.'

'Oh...?'

'Sure have.' He nodded. 'Guys pretending to be working for our paper, so they can have better access to information they need to work up a story... Then they have the balls to try and sell us the stuff they write.'

'I'm glad I've spoken to you,' I said. 'Now I'll know better than to give the guy the time of day.'

'Tell him to go take a hike in a latrine.'

Just then, the waitress appeared with our coffees. She placed them down on the table in front of us then disappeared again.

'About Javier Fontana,' I said. 'What exactly was he onto?'

Jorge Roig sighed, sat back in his chair. 'All I know is that he was investigating a lead he'd had...it was something to do with the Borrell family... Don't know if you've heard about them?'

I shook my head, sipped my coffee.

'Old Borrell was a rich art collector. Died last year and left his entire collection to a local state-owned gallery.'

'Didn't he have any kids?'

'Two daughters, if my memory serves me right.'

This sounded familiar, I thought. And said, 'Bet they were chuffed about that.'

'Oh, I bet.' He looked at me over the rim of his cup. 'The daughters disputed it and the house and art collection were held under a court order. But then the best pieces in the collection went missing.'

'So where are they?'

'That's anybody's guess... but Javier Fontana reckoned it was a sure bet the sisters had taken them.'

'So what was he doing down in Bardino, then?'

Roig's mouth rose in a lopsided grin. 'Look, Mister Blake,' he said.

'Blakey,' I corrected him.

'Sorry, Mr. Blakey... I don't know if you think I was born yesterday, but if so then maybe I ought to disabuse you.'

'No need to use the long words with me,' I told him. 'I'm just a private dick. Not one of your intellectual sorts.'

He zipped his lips together and gave me a look like I was a pile of numbers waiting to be added up. 'If Javier Fontana went down to Bardino, then it would have been because one or both of the sisters were down there,' he said. 'And you know that better than I do, Mr. Blakey, so can we cut the bullshit now?'

I looked at him and didn't say anything.

'If Javier wanted to speak to you,' Roig said, 'it must've been because you're working for one or other, or both of the Borrell sisters.'

'I'm afraid client confidentiality is everything in my line of work, Mr. Roig. It's a bit like the Hippocratic oath where doctors are concerned, I suppose, only more so.'

'I know, you already told me that.'

I shrugged. 'All I want is to get at the truth.'

'In that case we're both after the same thing, Mr. Blakey.' He took another sip of his coffee. 'Perhaps we could work together on this, favour each other with a little *quid pro quo…?*'

'Sure,' I said. 'Only problem is, I've already told you everything I know.' Much more to the point, I had the impression that Roig had told me everything he knew, and I didn't want him to rush to print. 'Listen, if you can hold fire on what we've talked about then I'd appreciate it.'

He shrugged. 'It's hardly worth printing, in itself. I mean there's the basis for a story there, and it could be a big one… But there are still far too many unknowns for me to want to rush to print.'

This was music to my ears. 'Okay,' I said, 'I'll tell you what. I'll give you the story as an exclusive, once I've got to the bottom of it, just so long as you promise to hold fire until it's over and tell me anything that you happen to turn up.'

'It's a deal.' I reached across the table and shook his hand. Then I took out a five-euro note and dropped it onto the table. 'That's for the coffees,' I said, and got up and went out.

48

I walked back to the car and drove to my hotel, found a place to park and went in and lay on the bed. So this Miguel Pascual character was no hack, I thought. Question was, who he was working for?

Whoever it was, they were after the Rembrandt. There could be no question about that. And they reckoned I'd be dumb enough to lead them to it. Well I wasn't as dumb as they reckoned.

Maybe it was Vince that sent the guy, I thought. Or Vicente Caportorio, to give the man his full name. Whoever he was, the would-be scribe was actually a mutt and he was sniffing where he shouldn't. Question was, what I was going to do about him.

I wondered about this for a while, and I was still wondering about it a little later when I was in the shower that was just along the hallway. The shower was about the only thing in the hotel that wasn't old and looking like it was about to fall apart, and the water came out nice and hot.

Dried, I went and dressed back in my room. Then I went out for a stroll through the narrow streets of the *Barrio Gogol*. Place had its own kind of atmosphere, I thought. All those old buildings with the louvered shutters. After a while, I found a place to eat. I had a plate of *lentejas* for the first course, followed by steak and chips. A cheap bottle of *tinto* came with the meal. The steak was thin as a miser's wallet and the wine was rougher than a thug's manners, but I was hungry and thirsty so I drank and ate it all anyway. And as I did so, I thought about the case. I thought about what had happened up till now, and what was likely to happen tomorrow. I planned out a course of action in my mind.

I showed at the Bar López at 2 p.m. the following afternoon, and sat at the same table I'd sat at the day before. The waiter came over and said, '*Buenos tardes*,' and I bade him good afternoon in return. 'It's quite a city you've got here,' I said.

'I expect you've been enjoying the many art treasures that Figarillo has to offer, *señor*.' His handlebar moustache rose in what I supposed must be a grin, but it didn't extend up as far as his eyes, which were watchful, I noticed.

'You're too right I have.' I smiled back at the man. 'Although I'd be enjoying myself a lot more if I could only purchase a certain Rembrandt that I've heard is currently on the market.'

The man nodded and lost his smile as he looked about him, to make sure nobody was within earshot. 'I have some news for you about that,' he said. 'If you'd like to come back here at five o'clock, I'll be able to set up a meeting with a man I know.'

'Does this man own the Rembrandt?'

'He is working for the owner, I believe.'

'Like an agent, you mean?'

'Something like that.'

'Okay.' I tried to think of a suitable location for what I had in mind. Of course, not knowing the city all that well didn't help. 'You know of any multi-storey car parks that are not too far away?'

The man smoothed down his tash as an aid to thought. 'There's one not all that far from here.'

'Can you print the name of the street it's on here for me?'

'Of course.'

He wrote on his pad, then tore the page off and gave it to me. I looked at what he'd written. The name of the street didn't mean anything to me. I folded the piece of paper and slipped it into my trouser pocket. 'I'll be back at five, then.' With that, I went back out without having eaten or drunk anything. I spotted the guy who was pretending to be a newspaper hack. He was sitting behind the wheel of his Seat Ibiza across the street.

He turned his head at that moment and seemed to notice me. I raised a hand in a sort of lazy salute, then I headed over to his car and climbed into the passenger seat. He looked at me and said, 'How's the shopping going?'

'Waiter's just given me an address to go to,' I said. 'Come along for the ride, if you want.'

'Sure. I appreciate it. I'll drive if you like.'

'Okay.'

'Where is it?'

I reached into my trouser pocket and brought out the piece of paper with the address of the multi-story car park written on it. 'Here,' I said and handed it to him.

He looked at it, then he looked at me. 'The waiter just give you this?'

'That's right.'

He screwed up his eyes as he scrutinized the paper. Then he nodded. 'Top of a multi-story car park,' he said. 'Bit of a strange place to go meet an art dealer, I should've thought.'

I shrugged. 'He said we're to meet the owner's agent first.'

'Maybe he'll take us to the other guy, is that it?'

'I dunno. I mean, I know as much as you do.'

'Waiter just wrote this down and gave it to you, and he didn't say anything else?'

'That's it.'

'Mm.'

'Well are you in on this or not?' I said. 'It's your call. I mean, you don't have to come if you don't want to.'

'No, I'm in on it, sure I am.'

'So let's get going, then.'

We set off through the busy city streets and the man seemed to know where we were headed so I left him to it. Minutes later, we arrived at the multi-storey car park. 'It's on the top floor,' I said.

'Private a place as any, I suppose.'

'Guess so.'

We entered the car park and climbed to the top. There were plenty of free parking spaces and he glided the Seat Ibiza into one of the empty bays. As he turned off the engine, I brought out my gun.

'What is this?' he said.

'You tell me.'

'I thought we were partners.' He looked genuinely upset and surprised. The guy was quite an acting talent gone to waste.

'What I thought, too,' I said. 'Till I found out you're not really a reporter at all.' I gave him my icepick smile. 'You see, I went to the offices of *La Vanguardia* and checked you out.'

He ditched the surprised and upset look.

'Who are you working for?' I said. 'Is it Vicente Caportorio?'

'Who?'

'Don't fuck with me, okay, because I'm just not in the mood.'

'I'm working alone.'

'Got your eyes on the Rembrandt, huh?'

'No, I'm a freelance reporter.'

It was always possible that he was telling the truth, but I couldn't take a chance on that. It would be too risky. 'I gave you the chance to play straight with me,' I said. 'Shame you didn't take it.'

'Look, I'm sorry I lied to you,' he said. 'But the truth is, a lot of people don't take you seriously if you tell them you're a freelance.'

'Get out of the car. And easy does it.'

I kept the gun pointed at him as I climbed out on my side. Or I tried to. But I was unsighted for a moment, as you always are in such circumstances, with the body of the car blocking your line of vision, and the mutt took the opportunity to bolt for it. He was skinny as a whippet and almost as fast as one, and he'd nearly reached the door to the stairwell by the time I spotted him. 'Hey, come back here,' I said. 'I need to talk to you.'

He glanced over his shoulder at me, then opened the door and went through it. I gave chase, but he'd already gone down two flights by the time I got to the door. I went after him, but he was nowhere to be seen by the time I got down to the street.

I'd handled the situation badly and could have kicked myself.

49

I returned to the Bar López for my appointment there at 5 p.m., and checked to see if there was any sign of the would-be hack or his Seat before I sat down. There wasn't, so far as I could see.

The waiter with the handlebar tash came over. '*Buenas tardes,*' he said. 'The man you have come to see is inside. If you'd like to come with me, I'll take you to him.'

'Sure.' I got up and followed the waiter into the café, our footsteps sounding as they struck the polished boards. The waiter led me through the long rectangular bar and past the horseshoe-shaped wooden counter. There were several tables right at the back, all of them empty save the one in the corner, and the waiter stopped at it. The man who was sitting there put his newspaper down and looked at us.

The waiter said, 'This is the *señor* who wanted to talk to you.'

The man nodded, then looked at me. 'Please take a seat.'

I parked myself on one of the upright wooden chairs and waited for the man to speak. He threw a look at the waiter, who got the message and took off, leaving us alone.

'I have been told that you have a taste for art treasures, *Señor* uh–'

'Ruiz,' I lied. 'Yes, that's so...'

'And you expressed an interest in buying a certain Rembrandt, I am told?'

'Indeed.'

The man continued to look at me, and he nodded almost imperceptibly as he did so, as if he were agreeing with some comment that had been whispered in his ear by an infinitesimally small elf in a voice so quiet as to be all but silent. He had shortish blond hair and blue eyes and was wearing newish jeans with a black Polo shirt and a camel-coloured suede jacket. He was a handsome son of a bitch, the sort you'd imagine the ladies would go for, and his face was vaguely familiar to me from somewhere. 'Who wouldn't want such a work on his wall?' he said. 'The question is of course, how much you want it.' He continued to look at me as if he were trying to weigh me up. 'Or to put it in slightly cruder terms, *Señor* Ruiz, how much you are willing or able to pay for it.'

'How much is the asking price?'

'Four million euros.'

'That's a lot of money.'

'The work we are talking about is a lot of painting, *Señor* Ruiz...it is a Rembrandt, after all.'

I acted as though I was trying to weigh the matter up in my mind for a moment, and then I said, 'Okay, four million it is.'

'You have the money?'

'I can get it, yes.'

'By when?'

'Tomorrow morning.'

'In that case, perhaps we should arrange a time and place where we can affect the sale and purchase of the painting.'

'The sooner the better, so far as I'm concerned.'

'Shall we say one p.m. tomorrow, then?'

'Fine with me.'

'Good... so if you'd like to give me your mobile number, I'll call you in the morning to tell you know where to come.'

'Sure.' I told him the number.

He called at just before twelve the following morning, and told me where to go and meet him. The address turned out to be a rundown block in one of the poorer parts of city. The flat was on the top floor. I went in through the front door and found myself in a dark and grimy lobby. I looked for the lift but there wasn't one, so I made for the stairs. When I got to the top, I found the door to the flat and pushed the buzzer. Somebody buzzed me in and, without saying a word, a big, shaven headed man frisked me, to checked that I wasn't armed. Finding that I wasn't, he said 'Follow me,' and led me along a dark hallway. He stopped outside a door and knocked once then entered, before he turned and beckoned me to follow.

Upon entering the room, I found myself looking at the man I'd spoken to in the Bar López the day before. He said hello and gave me a smile that was about as genuine as the Ray Bans they sell in the Chinese bazaars. He was wearing jeans with trainers and a navy Polo shirt today, and I'd worked out by now who he was and where I'd seen his face before.

'I'm so glad you could come, *Señor* Ruiz,' he said. Then he turned and went over to the fireplace and slid the Van Gogh lithograph that hung there to the side, to reveal a safe, and started moving the dial this way and that. He clearly knew the combination by heart, and opened the safe without bothering to listen for the clicks. Then he reached inside and brought out a small rectangular-shaped portrait. 'The Rembrandt that I believe you were interested in,' he said.

I examined the painting for a few moments, then I asked him how he had acquired the work. 'I inherited it,' he said, and I could almost have believed him were it not for the fact that I knew the painting had been stolen.

At that moment, the door opened and Inge Schwartz walked into the room. Or perhaps I should call her Barbara Borrell, seeing as that was her real name. She was holding a gun. '*Hola*, Arthur,' she said. 'I would introduce you both, but I see that you have already become acquainted.'

'But what are you doing here, Inge?' the man who was called Jaime asked. 'And what's with the gun?'

'Just a precaution,' she said. 'After you gave me the slip that last time, I figured I might need it.' She fixed him with a look that would have sunk a ship. 'I let myself in,' she said. 'I do hope you don't mind.'

'Where's Bruno?' I assumed he was referring to the hired muscle.

'He's working for me now,' she said. 'I made him an offer he found impossible to resist.'

'But this is all a big mistake,' Jaime said. 'I didn't mean to give you the slip. It's just that I've been rather busy just recently.'

'Oh I know you have. You've been rather busy stealing my Rembrandt and trying to sell it. Then once you'd done that you were planning on disappearing forever.'

'It's not yours but your father's and he left it to the state, so I don't see what you're getting on your high horse about.'

Inge shook her head in disgust and looked at me. 'It was Jaime here who waylaid you on the road outside of Magro, Arthur.'

'I rather guessed as much,' I said. 'So you set up the kidnapping of your sister with Jaime from the beginning, then he double-crossed you, is that it?'

'You're not as dumb as you look, Arthur.' She looked tearful all of a sudden. 'It wasn't meant to be like that,' she went on. 'Gisela wasn't supposed to get hurt. She was in on it with us, you see. Jaime had made contact with a couple of low life types who were supposed to carry out a false kidnapping for an agreed fee.'

'Are you saying he'd found a couple of goons who were going to pretend to kidnap Gisela and then let her go?'

'For a fee, yes, that's right.' She sighed. 'But that gangster Vince found out,' she went out. 'It was him or his henchmen who killed the two.'

'They killed Joaquim Gross and Juan Ribera, you mean?'

'Correct.'

'And I suppose it was Gross who provided you with the false German passports?'

She nodded. 'Then Vince kidnapped Gisela for real.'

'And that's when Jaime decided to go solo and ambush me and make off with the ransom, leaving Gisela with no hope, is that it?'

Inge's eyes were full of deadly poison and hatred. 'Exactly,' she said. 'Jaime killed her just as surely as that bastard Vince did.'

'So then you asked me to find the person who killed her and get your Rembrandt back, and you figured that you'd just follow me and see if I led you to Jaime.'

'I'm sorry that I used you in that way, Arthur,' she said. 'But you see, you were the only person I could really trust.'

I realized that I still loved her, despite everything. I told myself that I was a fool and that she'd been using me from the start. She'd taken me for a prize chump and I knew it; but somehow it didn't really seem to matter anymore. 'So now what?' I asked her.

'Jaime has to pay for his mistake.'

'You don't mean you're going to kill me, Barbara?' Jaime said.

'Murder's not your style, Inge,' I said. 'Or perhaps I mean Barbara.'

'It never was,' she agreed. 'But people change–and somebody has to make him pay for what he's done.'

'They'll lock you up and throw away the key,' Jaime said.

'Right now I really don't care all that much what happens to me.'

I cared. I cared a whole lot, even though I didn't think it would exactly have been politic to tell her as much. It was hardly the time or the place, after all.

I turned my head and looked at the man Inge/Barbara had come here to kill. I had of course recognized him from the first moment I set eyes on him in the flesh, as the man holding my client's hand in the photograph up on the wall in the bar I'd gone to in Magro that time. I remembered being insanely jealous of him when I'd seen him and Inge/Barbara together, looking so happy and in love. Well, so much for their great love. Jaime had cheated the two girls. Perhaps he was planning to have Inge/Barbara bumped off as well, so that he could make off with the Rembrandt and sell it someplace then keep the money all for himself.

A part of me was stunned to think that a man, any man, could give up the love of a woman like Inge Schwartz/Barbara Borrell for money, no matter how much of the stuff. Or for a Rembrandt, no matter how much it was worth. I just didn't know what to make of it. But then, I thought, there really was nothing as strange as people.

At that moment a voice said, 'Drop the piece,' and I turned my head abruptly. It was the man that had frisked me on the way in. He was holding a gun. Inge had reckoned she'd won him over to her side with the promise of a big payoff, but the man clearly had other ideas.

I tried to think of something to say to him. Something that might help persuade him that it wasn't such a good idea to shoot us both. No ideas sprang to mind.

Then the door opened and the guy who was passing himself off as Miguel Pasqual entered the room. Seeing Bruno turn to see who it was, I took a step towards him and kicked the gun out of his hand. Bruno jumped on my back as I moved to pick it up. He was a strong bastard, as you might expect, given that he was the hired muscle, and I was having a hard job getting him off me, but then a voice told him to quit the monkeying around and, to my surprise, he did so.

I turned and my heart sank once more as I saw the man who was passing himself off as Miguel Pasqual standing there with the gun in his hand. 'Get against the wall the three of you,' he said, and Bruno, Jaime and Inge/Barbara did as they were told.

He flashed me a sideways glance. 'Lucky for you I showed up in time, Arthur.'

'Don't tell me,' I said, 'it was Vince Caportorio who sent you here, right?'

He laughed. 'Trouble with you is, you don't ever trust anyone.'

'Who, then?'

'I was telling you the truth when I said I was a reporter after a story,' he said. 'The only part I lied about was when I said I was on the staff at *La Vanguardia*, because I'm actually a freelance.' He grinned. 'I purloined a press card that'd belonged to a Miguel Pasqual, a reporter with the newspaper, and have been operating under his name ever since. When I send stories out, I write them under my own name of course. I just use the alias to gain access to places and people. My real name's Javier Moreno.' He shrugged. 'I knew I had to follow you around if I was to have any hope of getting a story out of the whole business.'

I nodded slowly as I struggled to take it all in. Too many things had happened in too short a space of time, and my mind and senses were reeling. I looked over at Inge/Barbara and my heart went out to her. Okay, she hadn't exactly turned out to be as pure as the driven snow, but I'd never bought that act of hers anyway. It sounded like she'd only meant to find a way of reclaiming her lost inheritance, which wasn't really such a terrible thing to do after all. Or so it seemed to me at that moment, as I took out my mobile and called the police. Vince Caportorio and Jaime were the real villains of the piece, I told myself, as I listened to the ringtone.

Or was my readiness to believe Inge/Barbara's story only another sign of just how hopelessly in love with her I was, and what a fool I had become? I was still wondering about this, when the desk sergeant picked up and asked how she could help.

Dear reader,

We hope you enjoyed reading *Bad in Bardino*. Please take a moment to leave a review, even if it's a short one. Your opinion is important to us.

Discover more books by Nick Sweet at https://www.nextchapter.pub/authors/mystery-and-romance-author-nick-sweet.

Want to know when one of our books is free or discounted? Join the newsletter at http://eepurl.com/bqqB3H.

Best regards,
Nick Sweet and the Next Chapter Team

You might also like:
Switch by Nick Sweet

To read the first chapter for free, head to:
https://www.nextchapter.pub/books/switch

About the Author

Nick's crime novel, *The Long Siesta* (Grey Cells Press, the crime imprint of Holland House, September, 2015), was praised by a number of top crime authors, including Nicholas Blincoe, Caro Ramsay, Paul Johnston and Howard Linskey. Critic Barry Forshaw also wrote a positive review of the novel in *Crime Time* and followed up by giving Nick and his book a mention in *Brit Noir*, a guide to the best contemporary British crime writing and film.

Nick has also had stories included in prestigious anthologies in recent months, including *The Mammoth Book of Jack The Ripper Stories* (Little Brown, ed. Maxim Jakubowski) and *Sunshine Noir*. Nick's first crime novel, *Flowers At Midnight*, was published by Moonshine Cove, an American publisher, in 2012, and it was praised by the likes of Vincent Lardo and Quentin Bates. He has had around twenty short stories published in North American magazines, including *Descant* and the *Evergreen Review*.

So far, Nick's books can be divided up into crime novels, like *Bad In Bardino*, and works which are centred more on relationships, such as *One Flesh* - which focuses on a love tangle set in a Welsh mining village in the 1980s. Another of Nick's novels, *Young Hearts*, tells the story of a love triangle set against the backdrop of World War One, while *One Flesh* concerns itself with gay as well as heterosexual love.

Nick's crime novels can also be divided into different sub-categories. For instance, *Bad In Bardino*, is a PI novel set in Spain, and in this book, which is told in the first person, we see everything through the private detective's eyes; while *Switch* and *Only The Lonely*, both set in London, are shorter but pacy stories in which we see the action from different points of view – often through the eyes of the criminals. With *The Long Siesta*, a third-person narrative set in Seville, Nick again chose to tell the story so that all of the action is seen through the eyes of the main character, in this case Spanish police detective Inspector Jefe Velázquez.

Nick is British, but is currently living with his family in Fuengirola, Spain. Originally from Bristol, he studied at the universities of Cardiff and London, and lived for a long time in the English capital, where he ended up teaching English Literature and English Language in an FE college. He has moved around a fair bit, and has also lived and taught in Saudi Arabia, Abu Dhabi, Brighton, Barcelona, Bilbao and the city of Malaga. His experience of life in different places has helped his writing, and his books are set against a range of backdrops.

Nick has always taken a keen interest in sport, particularly in cricket and football, and he was a useful cricketer in his youth, having opened the batting regularly for Downend's first eleven in the Western League.

Nick speaks Spanish fluently and reads widely in both English and Spanish. If he had to choose his all-time favourite crime novels, then *The Long Goodbye* and *The*

Postman Always Rings Twice would both be up near the top of the list. Elmore Leonard's *Pronto, Get Shorty* or *Bandits* and Jim Thompson's *The Getaway* would also figure, as would Dashiell Hammett's *The Glass Key*. Nick also loves to read contemporary crime writers, to keep up with what his peers are doing, and is as likely to be found reading the latest Ian Rankin, Don Winslow or Lee Child, say, as rereading Tolstoy or Hemingway, or Don Quijote in the original Spanish.

Anyone who reads *One Flesh* and then goes on to read *Bad In Bardino* (or vice versa), might be excused for thinking these books must have been written by different authors, so different are they in terms not only of subject matter but also style. If so, then Nick would be happy with this state of affairs, because he feels that authors should try to keep their own personalities out of their books as far as possible.

Nick wants people to enjoy reading his books and keep turning the pages, and he would like to encourage satisfied readers to post reviews on Amazon or Goodreads, or wherever they see fit.